Praise for

Were Chronicles

Ms. Smith has begun a fast paced and compelling series with this story that grabs the reader from the start. ~ *Fallen Angel Reviews*

I recommend Pack Alpha by Chrissy Smith. It is a good read that incorporates an intense, sexy alpha male with lots of believable sexual tension... This story makes me wish that I had my own alpha.
~ *Two Lips Reviews*

Displaying a sometimes uncomfortable grip on your emotions Pack Alpha is sure to require a box of tissues... With a whole cast of lovable secondary characters I can't wait to see what Crissy Smith comes up with next for the world of the Were Chronicles series. ~ *Veiled Secrets Reviews*

Step into Crissy Smith's world of werewolves with her new release, Pack Alpha – you will enjoy every single word! ~ *Joyfully Reviewed*

If you enjoy fiery heroines and hot alpha males who will fight for what is theirs than this book is for you. I for one will be looking for more from this author. Hopefully we can hear more from the rest of the pack.
~ *Whipped Cream Erotic Reviews*

Reviewer Top Pick! When I read the blurb about this book, I knew I wanted to read it and it didn't disappoint… With all the different Packs, this could be a very long running series that will be sure to delight its readers. *~ Night Owl Romance Reviews*

You will not want to miss this exciting new series from author, Crissy smith. I loved Gage's Alpha attitude, and Marissa's independent, "I will do what I want", outlook. *~ Paranormal Romance Reviews*

Total-E-Bound Publishing books by Crissy Smith:

Corporate Wolves
The Favour
Losing Control

Secrets
The Shifter and the Dreamer

Seduced by the Neighbour
Lacey's Seduction
Eternal
Bid High
Fated Love
Vamps in the City

Anthologies
Caught in the Middle: Magical Ménage

Seasonal Collections
Bite Me: Savage Love
Summer Seductions: Summers' Girl
Cloaks and Daggers: Vapmire Hunter

WERE CHRONICLES
Volume One

Pack Alpha

Pack Enforcer

Pack Territory

CRISSY SMITH

Were Chronicles Volume One
ISBN # 978-1-78184-602-5
©Copyright Crissy Smith 2009
Cover Art by Natalie Winters ©Copyright 2009
Interior text design by Claire Siemaszkiewicz
Total-E-Bound Publishing

Published in 2013 by Total-E-Bound Publishing, Think Tank, Ruston Way, Lincoln, LN6 7FL, United Kingdom.

.

PACK ALPHA

Dedication

To my husband and daughter who let me be myself
and dream my dreams

Chapter One

Marissa took a drink of the coffee she'd picked up at the last gas station. The hot liquid burned her tongue and tasted like slug. It wasn't Starbucks that was for sure. She had flown into the Texas International Airport and rented a car to drive the rest of the way to the small town her sister called home. Her mind was busy thinking about how her sister Elizabeth had been so excited about moving here, but looking at the passing scenery of trees, trees, and more trees, Marissa didn't get it. It was so big and wide. No buildings, other cars, or people around.

Rolling her window down and turning Bon Jovi even louder on the stereo, she concentrated on the drive — not the reason for coming. She dreaded going into Pack territory, but Elizabeth was the only family she had left, and after finding her mate, Elizabeth wanted Marissa there for the mating ceremony.

That thought brought a smile to Marissa's face as she glanced at the invitation on the seat next to her. She wanted Elizabeth to be happy, and Greg sounded like a nice guy. She'd spoken to him numerous times on the phone, and he'd always been respectful towards her. And that wasn't common. A were who couldn't shift was an outsider. And everyone except Elizabeth had treated her that way her entire life.

Marissa had left the Pack she'd been raised in as soon as she could. Never to step foot on any Pack territory again. That was until later today. Elizabeth, on the other hand, had stayed until she met Greg, a member of a different Pack. After the initial meeting, he had offered her a teaching position at the elementary school and she had taken it. He had been courting her ever since with the blessing of her new Pack Alpha, Gage Wolf.

Marissa chuckled, thinking of everything Greg had done to win her sister's heart. He'd known he wanted Elizabeth and had patiently waited. It had taken Elizabeth a year to agree to the mating ceremony, but she finally did. Marissa knew one of the reasons Elizabeth had been holding off was because of her.

Marissa had the same instincts as any other were and with that came the need of a Pack, but she had given up on that a long time ago. She'd grown up alone and would always remain that way. In the middle between a shifter and a human. She had many gifts due to her genes—the extended life span, the wolf traits, and some enhanced features—but not enough.

But Marissa would put everything she had into this week and the ceremony that meant so much to her sister.

The differences between her and Elizabeth had grown as they had aged. That was why Marissa had never visited Elizabeth's new home. She wasn't scared being in Pack territory; she just didn't want to face all the males and their egos. And from what she understood, the Pack's Alpha or leader was pretty young himself.

When around other wolves, the female wolf inside her demanded she mate with one of her own kind. So, as long as she avoided everyone except her sister as much as she could and kept her urges inside, everything would be okay. She would not act like the wolf she couldn't shift into.

And if the Alpha was anything like her old one, she'd just tell him where to stick it. The idea of telling the Alpha of a territory to go to hell made her smile wider and laugh harder. She wasn't seventeen anymore. She wasn't a scared little girl who had to follow everything someone told her. No, she was a grown woman. And she was going to enjoy the time with her sister.

She wasn't dressed to impress the Alpha or any men in the territory as she currently wore a pair of hip-hugging jeans and a tight pink T-shirt. The paint on her toe nails matched the colour of her shirt, as did the flip-flops. It was a far cry from the suit she wore everyday as an office assistant. She felt free.

When she almost missed the turn off to the territory gate and turned the car sharply to the left, the back of the car skidded around and kicked up dirt. Laughing, she straightened the car and slowed her speed. She didn't think Gage Wolf would be happy if she took out a couple of trees.

When she reached the gate, she stopped and waited for the guard. He didn't disappoint. A man over six feet came over to the window and leaned down, smiling at her.

"Can I help you?" he asked in a husky voice.

She took a deep breath and smiled back. If all the men were this good-looking, she had her work cut out for her trying to keep her distance. They'd flirt and tease with her, and she had to be strong and resist, because as soon as they knew her secret, she wouldn't exist any longer to them. And no matter what she said to herself, the rejection always hurt.

"I'm Elizabeth Boyd's sister. I need directions to her house please."

His smile didn't change and he nodded. "Give me just a minute." He winked, then headed to the guardhouse and picked up the phone.

No doubt checking with the Alpha to make sure she could come in and play. With her own sister, no less, Marissa thought bitterly.

She kept her face friendly and thoughts to herself as he came back to the car. "Problem?"

"Not at all," he said, shaking his head, and gave her directions to her sister's house. "My name's Steve if you want to get together later," he added.

Not in this life. "Hmm, we'll see." She was careful not to commit to anything he could hold her to later. The laws of the Pack were much different than the laws where she lived. Marissa knew them all and had only ever broken one.

Shaking that unpleasant thought from her head, she drove through the gate. Looking back into the rear view mirror, she saw Steve standing with a smile on his face.

"Down, girl," she told herself. "This is Pack territory."

* * * *

Gage Wolf hung up the phone in his study and glanced at the clock. Elizabeth's sister had made good time. When Elizabeth had told him she wanted her sister here for the ceremony, he'd thought it was a good idea.

He remembered the conversations he'd had with Elizabeth about her sister when he was first considering accepting Elizabeth into his Pack.

Elizabeth was protective and worried about her younger sibling. He understood it must have been hard for a non-shifter to grow up, but he didn't get why Marissa refused to see her sister.

And that, he knew, was the main reason Elizabeth had held back on the ceremony for so long. Gage was determined to not allow Marissa to hold her sister back from what Elizabeth wanted. And she wanted Greg.

He looked up at the knock on his door. His second-in-command, Logan, poked his head in. "I'm taking off now."

Gage nodded.

"Want to go for a run later?" Logan asked as he opened the door wider to lean against the jamb.

"I'll be going by the Boyd house tonight," Gage told him, watching his friend and Pack member smile.

"I don't think you'll be the only one."

"What do you mean?"

The mischievous twinkle in his eyes was unmistakable. "Steve might have mentioned to a few of the guys how hot she is."

Gage shook his head. Steve hadn't wasted any time if Logan already knew. Gage didn't need any more complications. "She's not here to mate."

Logan laughed. "Well, that may be beside the point."

"She doesn't need to be bothered."

"Well, who is to say it would bother her. She is a were."

"Yes but still…" Gage trailed off. He wasn't sure why he already felt protective towards her. His best guess would be that Elizabeth had shared the secret of her sister not being able to shift and how it still affected her. While it wouldn't be a problem to his Pack members, he didn't want the girl hurt further by rejection.

"Well, then you might want to get over there." With that, Logan turned and left.

Cursing, Gage stood. He needed to set the ground rules down for this woman.

Gage walked up to Elizabeth's attractive two-storey house a few minutes later. Before he could ring the bell, the door opened and a young pack member stepped out onto the porch.

Gage stepped aside to let the man pass. Jeff looked surprised to see him before quickly dropping his eyes.

"Alpha."

Gage nodded his hello and stepped into the open doorway and right into the middle of a conversation in progress.

"I'm going upstairs to unpack. If you have any more visitors, tell them to come back in a week."

Elizabeth stood with her back to him, her hands clasped tightly behind her. It only took a few seconds for her to realise he was there, because she turned and faced Gage with a surprised look on her face.

"Gage," she greeted and he wasn't certain if it was in welcome or not. He could practically feel the tension coming off of her. "I didn't know you were coming by. I mean, I thought you might, but with some many…" She trailed off, looking nervously around her.

He only lifted an eyebrow. "I take it you've had a lot of guests?"

Elizabeth didn't look amused. "Yeah, and it's driving her crazy. I'm sorry. I don't know where my manners are. Please come in."

Gage entered the living room, immediately taking in the new scent and the others mixed in with it. He could have named the wolves who had stopped by. There was only one smell he didn't recognise, and that had to be Elizabeth's sister.

His nostrils flared as he took in the new scent. The fresh wood and spice smell of the newcomer had his body immediately coming to life. He knew that if her scent was so strong he was going to have his hands full keeping the available wolves away from her.

"I'll go get Marissa."

Gage laid a gentle hand on her arm. "I'll go up. I need to talk to her privately."

Elizabeth looked uncertain for a moment, shifting on her feet and looking upstairs.

"I just want to welcome her, tell her a few things about the ceremony, and make sure she understands some Pack rules."

Elizabeth nodded. Gage knew she was worried about not only her sister but him also.

"She...she's not always the nicest." Elizabeth looked away when she said it, and Gage knew it wasn't easy for her to be in between her sister and her Alpha.

Gage smiled and patted her arm. "Don't worry. We'll both be fine," Gage assured her.

That seemed to console Elizabeth, and she nodded. "I'll just be in the kitchen starting dinner then."

Gage listened as he made his way upstairs. He had heard the woman's annoyed comment while he stood at the door. He could also hear her muttering to herself from the far bedroom.

He walked into the bedroom and stopped in his tracks. It was one of the most amazing sights he'd ever seen—her butt was sticking out from under the bed with her legs tucked under her. She moved from side to side and felt himself growing hard.

He growled at the reaction, and she must have heard because there was a bang against the bottom of the bed, which was followed by a stream of curses.

She peered out from under the bed, then crawled out, rubbing her head.

"What the hell are you doing in here?" she demanded.

"I was going to ask you the same thing. Do you always crawl under beds?"

Marissa gave him the once over. Her attraction was immediate—he could sense it. Gage could hear her heart beat pick up and watched as she wiped nervous hands on her pants. She shifted from foot to foot and he could smell her arousal. The stubborn look on her face told him she was going to fight it.

"Gage Wolf?" Even though he was certain she knew exactly who he was, she phrased it as a question.

Gage nodded at the beauty in front of him. To say he was taken by surprise was an understatement. Where Elizabeth was pale and slender with blue eyes and blonde hair, her sister looked nothing like her.

For one thing, she was scowling at him even though he could smell her desire. She had long dark hair and crystal green eyes that were narrowed. It was quite obvious she didn't like her attraction to him, but he couldn't say the same. It had been a very long time since he'd felt this instant hunger.

"I am," he answered her unnecessary question. "And you are Marissa."

Marissa nodded, trying to swallow past the lump in her throat. His voice was deep and she could almost feel it wrapping around her. This reaction wasn't good and she needed to get herself under control.

He was absolutely, positively the best looking man she had ever seen. He was taller than she was — she'd guess over six-two. He wore black slacks and a button down shirt with the sleeves rolled up.

"Is there something you needed?" she asked, crossing her arms over her chest.

Gage followed the gesture with his eyes, and Marissa blushed when she realised she had just brought more attention to herself.

"I came to welcome you to my territory as is proper for any Pack Alpha," Gage said, taking a step closer. "And to go over some rules."

Marissa stiffened at his words. She shouldn't be surprised. She could guess what rules he was going to make sure she knew. She'd heard them all her life. Even steeling herself for them didn't keep the hurt out.

"You were raised in a Pack?" he asked.

Marissa nodded, though she knew he already knew the answer. Elizabeth already told her that Gage knew about her differences.

"I don't expect things will be such different here."

Marissa didn't either. "I understand," she said, stiffening her shoulders and fisting her hand at her side.

"Do you have any questions for me on how to behave?"

The pep talk she had given herself on the drive allowed her to speak calmly. "No, I don't believe I have any questions on my behaviour here. I assure you that I have no interest in your Pack. One week —

seven days—I'll be here. I think you can deal with it as I have to. Then I'll be gone and you won't have to worry about me corrupting your precious Pack."

When she finished, something like surprise crossed his face briefly, and he growled. No one had probably ever spoken to him that way before. But Marissa wasn't going to be intimidated.

When he took a step closer, she could sense the anger from him.

"I'll warn you once about the way you talk to me. I don't know how your Alpha reacted, but that kind of disrespect will not be tolerated here."

Marissa didn't tell him that she'd never been brave enough to talk to her old Alpha like that. Marissa backed up as the Alpha stepped closer.

"Also, I know how long you are here for. I know a selfish woman like you wouldn't give up more than a week for the sister who loves her and has waited far too long to be happy because of her."

His words stopped her retreat. "Selfish? You just called me selfish."

Even with the smile that touched his lips, he didn't look any less furious. "I did."

"Well, let me tell you something, Mr. Wolf. I wouldn't be here if I didn't love my sister. I wouldn't set foot on this territory if it had not meant so much to Elizabeth. I gave my blessing to her a long time ago." Marissa took a deep breath as she wound down. She realised she was explaining herself to him, and not wanting to give him an information he could use on her later, she quickly tried to cover her outburst. "Not that it's any of your business."

Marissa backed up until she felt the wall at her back, and Gage closed the distance between them.

"You do know who I am. My status here?"

Marissa didn't trust the smooth smile or easy tone. "Yes."

"So are you trying to piss me off? Any intelligent person would know better than to tell an Alpha a Pack member wasn't his business or make the comments as you have." When he reached forward and grabbed her arm, it was too fast for Marissa to avoid. "I feel sorry for the troubles you must have given to your Pack Leader."

The electricity that flowed through Marissa's body at Gage's touch drew a startled breath from her. He must have felt it too, because he immediately let go of her. Marissa stared at him as neither spoke for several minutes. She grasped at anything she could say to make him go away.

"I don't have a Pack Leader. But I do know how to address the Alpha of a Pack who had been kind enough to let me visit. I apologise. My attitude and disrespectful comments were uncalled for." Fear and uncertainly had her lowering her eyes to the floor in a submissive gesture. It galled her to show any submission to him, but his touch unnerved her.

She could feel his stare even though she wasn't looking at him and barely stopped herself from shifting on her feet. The urge to run coursed strongly through her body.

When he finally spoke, she was so surprised her eyes met his.

"Very well then. Now I believe your sister in downstairs about to have a fit with us up here arguing so I suggest we finish this another time."

Marissa nodded, relieved he would leave now. Maybe he was just as unsettled as she was.

Gage took his leave without another word to her. Marissa sat on her bed and thought about what had just taken place. She looked up at a sound in the hall, she saw Elizabeth standing at the entrance of her guestroom with wide eyes and a frown.

"Don't start," Marissa warned her sister.

Elizabeth shook her head. "Gage is a nice man and a good Alpha."

Marissa smiled even though she felt her face wanted to crack. "I'm sure he is," she lied.

Chapter Two

Gage wasn't surprised at the knock on his office door, though it did annoy him. Logan opened the door and walked in without hesitation. He grinned at Gage as he sat and lounged on the couch.

"What?" Gage asked, not in the mood for any more games tonight.

"Sam said he ran into you after you met with the Boyd woman." Logan paused for dramatic effect. It was something Gage usually found amusing. Tonight wasn't one of those times. "He said you seemed agitated."

Gage snorted in response. "I am not agitated."

Logan nodded, his expression growing serious. "No, I didn't think so. If you were agitated, you might be pacing your office liked a caged…wolf."

Gage didn't miss the twitch in Logan's lips. His second kept the smile from his face this time, but barely. "I am not pacing."

"No. Absolutely no pacing going on here." Logan agreed too easily, proving that he was finding too much humour with his Alpha.

"I have had enough with foolish talk for one night, so knock it off." Gage barely kept the growl out of his voice.

Logan's blue eyes sparkled. "Things didn't go so well with Elizabeth's sister, I take it?"

Gage snorted again and went back to pacing. "She's rude, stubborn, and..."

"Beautiful?"

Gage swirled around. "How do you know she's beautiful?"

To Logan's benefit, he kept a straight face. Logan only gave a careless shrug. "A lot of the men were quite impressed with her."

"She is not here to be hit on by every available male in the territory," he said strongly. Too strongly even to his own ears.

"Well, since she was raised in a Pack, I don't think we should have too much trouble with her," Logan predicted. No doubt trying to be helpful.

Gage didn't respond.

"Being raised in a Pack she already knows most rules and our laws," Logan continued.

"Oh, she knows the rules all right. Knows how to ignore them."

Logan nodded as if he understood. "It's not the first time you have encountered a rogue or undisciplined wolf. What makes her different?"

That question was what was bothering Gage. "I don't know, but get me everything you can on her."

Logan stood and left Gage once again alone in his office.

"Let's see what secrets you have, Marissa Boyd," he said quietly.

* * * *

After dinner, Marissa claimed being tired from her trip and locked herself in her room. Elizabeth's future mate had joined them for dinner and Marissa had to admit she liked him even more than she thought she would.

It was obvious that he only had eyes for Elizabeth. He had kept looking at her with stars in his eyes. Marissa didn't miss the subtle touches that passed between the two of them either.

Marissa was thrilled for her sister, but there was just a hint of jealousy down deep. She tried to push it away, but it was there—just as it had always been.

Deciding a bath would soothe her, Marissa filled the tub with hot water and relaxed into the marble enclosure. Her sister's house was nice. It wasn't too fancy but very homey. She thought it matched her sister just as this territory seemed to match her.

Marissa sighed, thinking about the territory. She had been shocked when the Alpha Gage hadn't demanded she leave. She had been rude to him. She didn't know of any other Alpha who wouldn't have punished her.

And he would have had every right. She was his guest and was expected to follow his rules. It might have been more complicated if she had a Pack Alpha standing for her, but she had no one. She didn't have anyone in her corner and help her smooth things over with him.

Thinking about Gage had her temperature rising. Oh, he was a good-looking man, although there was more to him than just that. There was power there— that was unmistakable—but she sensed something different in him then her old Alpha. Even though they had argued, she didn't have the same fear of his power as she did others in his position. It was like she could feel the compassion inside him for others. That could only lead to trouble.

She'd given her heart once to a wolf, and it had ended badly. Very badly. She wouldn't repeat that mistake. Although the Alpha was tempting. So very tempting that Marissa found herself rubbing her breasts thinking about him.

This wasn't a normal reaction for her. She could always resist her urges. The wolf inside her might not like it, but she could do it. Her only fear was that Gage could push past her defences and make her vulnerable.

As she dipped a hand under the water and rubbed the ache between her legs, she made a vow to herself right then and there. She would never be vulnerable again. Even if it left her sexually frustrated.

She let her fingers rub over the swollen folds of her sex before dipping inside. The pressure of two fingers entering felt so good. With her other hand, she pulled and pinched her nipple. The slight pain added to her arousal.

As she closed her eyes, it was Gage's face that popped into her head. What would he do if he walked in and saw her touching herself?

Weres were very sexual, and Marissa had stronger urges than most women she knew. Her friends back home were fully human so they wouldn't understand the burning she constantly felt.

Would Gage drop to his knees beside her? Place his hand with hers? Pump his thick fingers inside her?

Marissa let out a low long moan at the thought. Her fingers moved easily between the folds of her core, building the release she needed. She wondered what he looked like without his clothes. His tanned arms had been revealed earlier. Even with his clothes, she could tell he was built. She'd bet he had a wonderful body.

Fingers moving faster, Marissa lifted her hips as she finally reached her climax. Biting her lip, she came slowly but fully with thoughts of Gage teasing her.

* * * *

Gage stared at the information in front of him. "They just let her go?" he asked, looking over to Logan.

The other man glanced up from the pages he was reading. "Apparently."

Gage shook his head. "Something's wrong here. They didn't even try to keep track of her."

Logan placed the papers he had in his hands on the sofa next to him. "This is not telling us anything. It leads to more questions than answers. You need to talk to this girl again."

Gage nodded as he looked past Logan to the window in his office. Thoughts of Marissa Boyd had kept him up last night. The full moon was only six nights away, and every wolf got distracted as it came closer, but he was more than just *distracted* by this woman. If the hard-on he was sporting was any indication, he needed to do more with her than just talk. It'd been years since he'd felt this hot for any woman.

"Alpha?"

Snapping his head up, he didn't miss the amusement all over Logan's face. "I'll go talk to her."

"Elizabeth should still be teaching, so you should have all morning alone…so you can talk privately."

Gage barely contained his groan. Not only had he been hard since first seeing this woman, but it seemed his Beta was determined to get him together with her.

"I'm just going over to talk to her," Gage stood, stretching his back from sitting too long at his desk.

"Of course, Alpha," Logan agreed, not bothering to hide his huge grin as he left Gage's office.

If he didn't satisfy himself with Marissa, maybe he would come back to the house and take Logan down a few notches. That wouldn't take care of the most pressing problem but it might make him feel better.

He had a feeling that any amount of time spent with Marissa was going to test his control.

Marissa stood on her sister's back porch, looking out at the woods that surrounded the house. It was so beautiful here.

She remembered a time when she hated having to be around crowds. In the time since she'd left her Pack, she had gotten used to people and the noise. What she had once hated now served the purpose of keeping her from having to admit that she'd never have what her sister did.

They used to stay up late talking in the room they shared about the perfect place to make a home. This territory was everything they'd wanted growing up and Elizabeth had finally found it.

Back then, Marissa still had hope that one day the Pack would accept her. She no longer carried that hope. It had been replaced by the bitterness that she didn't belong anywhere. Even as the wind called for the wolf to run, she couldn't.

The thick green grass cushioned her bare feet as she stepped onto it. The wolf inside moved restlessly to be let out. Her skin prickled and she shivered. The wolf needed to be released. Normally she would do this with sex, but this was not the place. It was going to be a painful and agonising week.

Moving farther away from the porch towards the edge of the trees, Marissa felt her wolf jump inside her skin. God, how she wished she could shift. Could let the wolf completely free like it wanted, like it needed.

But that wasn't going to happen. She couldn't shift and no one had figured out how or why this happened to some. Her DNA was not like her sister's or a mortal human's. She was caught somewhere in the middle.

Resigned and unhappy, she turned back towards the house and stopped short when she noticed the man who stood on porch watching her. Her wolf growled its approval, demanding she take this available male.

Gage watched as Marissa's eyes widened. She licked her lips, and his cock jumped in his jeans. He'd been surprised to find her staring into woods like she was ready to go running. He didn't know much about non-shifters. They were not common. Only a handful of them existed. But the intensity of her stare was like that before a shift.

He quickly covered the distance between them. Marissa didn't move away from him when he reached her. Her green eyes had started to glow.

"The wild calls to you?"

She nodded and licked her lips again.

"How does it make you feel? Not being able to shift?" He wanted to know more about her. He wanted to reach the woman, and the wolf, under the skin.

She looked so sad he wanted to wrap his arms around her and tell her everything would be okay.

She cleared her throat twice before speaking. "Trapped."

She had started shaking and he reached for her. "Does it hurt?" He couldn't imagine how it would feel for his wolf to be trapped.

When she only shrugged a shoulder, he continued, "What can I do?"

Her gaze met his before dropping to his lips. When she sucked her bottom lip, he felt the last thread of his resolve slipping. Yanking her to him, he took control of her mouth. She didn't fight him, but opened immediately. He plunged his tongue inside, dominating the kiss. Her low moan only drove him on farther, harder. With one hand wrapped in her hair, holding her head still, he used the other to bring their bodies closer.

Her lips moved against his. Her hands clawed at the shirt on his back. Knowing she was as out of control as he was amazing.

It seemed there was much more to this woman than he had thought. With one kiss he was afraid he had become addicted. She tasted like heaven.

She yanked at the soft black shirt he wore.

He moved his mouth to her neck where he nibbled the sensitive flesh.

"Yes," she encouraged. "Yes." Kneading the muscles on his back. Dragging her nails down painfully.

Gage hissed before lifting her so she could wrap her arms and legs around him, letting her rub against the steel rod hidden by jeans.

"Please." She rubbed herself harder against him. "Please."

Gage knew he should stop the mating before it went too far, but he didn't. It wasn't his wolf in control, but the man. And the man wanted this woman under him naked, bucking, begging, and the wolf was urging him on.

"Oh God. I'm burning for you. Please." Marissa's mouth was everywhere on him. He could swear he felt her canines lengthen as she licked and sucked his neck.

Hitching her higher around his waist, he walked deeper into the trees. They would give him plenty of cover as he took this woman.

Chapter Three

Marissa felt her back meet the grass as Gage laid her down. His weight quickly covered her, sending electric currents through her body.

His eyes met hers briefly before he reclaimed her mouth. This kiss wasn't as forceful as the last, but more coaxing. As if he was trying to get her body to trust his. Her body didn't care about trust—it just wanted him hard and fast.

When his mouth started to trail down, she took the opportunity to pull off his torn shirt. She yanked the remaining material from his body. He sat up between her legs and she felt his gaze burn into her as he slowly lifted the T-shirt she had dressed in earlier. He had more control, more patience than she did, and when Marissa raised her hand to help, he slapped it away.

"Mine," he growled at her.

Marissa tried to close her legs in hope of relieving the ache between them, but he only spread his knees wider moving her legs with him. If she had been naked, she would have been spread out wide for him. The way she wanted to be.

"Gage. Now. Please now."

He bent his head and smiled at her. "Giving the Alpha orders, little one?" He ran his tongue over the silky cup of her bra. "You shall be punished for that."

When he licked one hard nipple through the silk, Marissa's body jerked. "Oh please."

Running his teeth over the opening clasp of her bra, he chuckled. "You will beg, little one. Before I am finished, you will beg." He used his teeth to tear open her bra.

Marissa thought she might explode right there when his hot moist mouth covered her nipple. She lifted her hands to the back of his head to hold him to her. Her body screamed for more.

Without removing his mouth, he grabbed her hands and placed them over her head. "Keep your hands there," he told her before moving to the other breast and nipple.

Marissa tried—she really did—but when his body started moving down hers, her hands automatically to his shoulders. Gage growled and nipped at her wrist. The sharp pain had her gasping and arching into him at the same time. He placed her hands back over her head and gave her a stern look, before trailing his tongue down her body.

Liquid fire slid over her, around her, and in her. Marissa desperately tried to grab onto anything to keep her hands still. Clawing at the grass and dirt, she dug her hands in, trying to anchor herself. She'd never felt this hot, this needy. He was torturing her.

Skipping the cotton shorts she wore, Gage slowly brought one of her legs up and ran his tongue behind her knee. Her moans told him what she liked. He followed the path from her knee to the edge of her shorts.

"Yes. Yes," she repeated over and over, her head moving from side to side.

Gage slowly started to peel the shorts off. The crotch was wet and he paused to smell.

"Little wolf is dripping for me," he said, his husky voice in contrast to his slow exploration. He wanted her, she knew that. But he was taking his sweet time.

"Yes. Yes, I am," she admitted.

He pulled her shorts all the way off and threw them behind him. With a gentle touch, he ran one finger over the crotch of silk panties. The only barrier left on her. "Wet. So wet and hot."

Leaning over, he closed his mouth over the silk and sucked. Then, with a quick yank, removed them.

"Oh. God. Oh. Please." Marissa moved her legs together to hold him in place.

Pressing both hands on her thighs, he opened them back up. "Do you not have any control over your body?" he teased. "Hold still."

Hold still? Was he joking? She was going to go insane.

He pulled away from her enough for her to see him.

"Don't stop!" she demanded, desperate to feel him inside her.

Lifting that elegant eyebrow, Gage gave her an annoyed look. "Orders again? You just can't help yourself, can you?"

Before she could respond, Marissa found herself flipped and on all fours. She dug her hands and knees into the ground. "Yes. I mean, no. I mean...please just take me."

Marissa felt his arousal through his rough jean material as he leaned his body over hers. "Is this what you want?"

"Yes. Oh please, yes."

Gage's hand left her, and he released himself from the confines of his jeans. He ran his hands down her flank and over her curves, pressing his naked body against hers. Marissa almost yowled in pleasure.

Marissa arched for him. If she could just get him inside... She started to reach back with one hand.

"No. Don't move," he ordered.

She screamed in frustration, but he only laughed at her.

"No control." Placing a kiss in the small of her back, he pulled away again.

Marissa turned her head to complain and was shocked by the feel of his hand on her ass.

Smack.

"Ahhhhhhhhh." Bracing herself with her hands, Marissa trembled. "What?"

"Need to learn manners." *Smack.*

Marissa cried out again.

"Need to learn restraint." *Smack. Smack.*

"I...what...No!"

"Someone should have taught you to follow orders a long time ago." *Smack.*

Tears formed in her eyes. Marissa had never been treated like this. This wasn't some sex game. This was real—punishment—and it hurt. And it felt good. How could it feel good? She'd never been one to enjoy pain with sex, but with Gage, it seemed to fit perfectly.

Gage landed three more slaps with his hand. She lifted up each time, meeting his hand. The sharp pain only made her hotter. Made her hungrier for him. She'd never been spanked in her life. Her clit throbbed. She could taste blood from where she was biting her lip. Her mind filled with emotions she didn't understand but didn't really care about.

He stopped spanking her and rubbed his hands over her ass. As he slipped a finger between her folds, she couldn't hold back a moan. He thrust his finger inside before pulling out and positioning himself behind her.

One hand drove into her hair and he yanked her head back as he plunged inside her willing body. He filled her completely with the first thrust, causing her to scream. She hadn't gotten a good look at his cock before, and she now knew that he was well endowed.

As he moved in and out with deep slow strokes, Marissa felt her body stretch to accommodate him but the stretch felt amazing. Each time he pushed into her body, she slammed herself back to meet each thrust.

Their rhythm flowed like a dance as the speed picked up and he rode her harder. She kept her head bent and her eyes tightly closed and tried to hang on to the magical feeling of belonging. Both of his hands now held her hips tightly as his strokes grew shorter and more desperate. Unable to hold out any longer, Marissa lifted her head and cried out into the wild as her orgasm ripped through her body.

"Yes. Let me hear you," he told her, pounding inside harder.

Three more thrusts and he exploded inside her, releasing his seed deep inside and taking her through completion once again.

Marissa gained all her senses back slowly. The grass which she had collapsed on was wet, but she hadn't noticed earlier. Her cheek rested in a patch of dirt that her hands had clawed at earlier.

The weight of Gage, while heavy, was comforting. Breathing in, she held his masculine scent. When he started to lift off her, she barely held back a sigh at the loss of his warmth. Gage fell onto his back, but she kept her eyes closed. Her hair was probably messed and she no doubt had a sleepy, satisfied look.

He surprised her when he reached over and covered her shapely bottom with his palm. "You okay?"

"Uh huh."

Damn if she didn't sound content and relaxed even to her own ears. The tension in her body seemed to have disappeared completely. When Gage leaned over and replaced his hands with his lips, she couldn't find any reason to tell him to stop. Being with him had been the best sexual experience of her life.

Her eyes were still closed when, using the lightest pressure, he nipped then licked at her skin. Then awareness slammed back into her.

Her eyes flew open and she lifted her head. "You *spanked* me!"

Throwing one arm over her legs to hold her in place as she tried to turn over, Gage said, "So I did."

Marissa shook her head at him. "But…you spanked me."

Continuing to run circles over her with the tip of his tongue, he grunted his agreement.

Heat followed Gage's tongue as it traced along her body. What was going on with her? What was going on with *him*? He had to realise he had just mated with a non-shifter. She knew some Packs mated with humans and some kept it hidden, but she didn't know of one who would risk openly mating with a non-shifter. And he was the Pack Alpha!

Marissa jerked away so quickly that, in his surprise, Gage released her.

Once on her feet, she began to look around desperately for her clothes. Her shirt was next to Gage's hand. She didn't think the house was too far away, so maybe no one would see her if she ran quickly.

Gage sat, looking up at her. He watched her as if he knew she wanted to run from him. But while she going into full panic mode, he looked like it pissed him off.

"This what you're looking for?" He held the T-shirt out to her.

Marissa nodded and dropped her eyes. The wolf inside Gage would acknowledge the submission, but the man might not be so easily fooled.

"Well, come and get it," he challenged.

Marissa took a careful step to him. She just got within arm's length of him and leaned forward to grab the shirt, and damn, if he didn't grab her first. He turned quickly, holding both wrists, until she was on her back.

Following her first instinct, Marissa wiggled and fought. He only pressed more of his weight down and growled at her.

"Stop fighting me and stop moving around. I'm not hurting you," he told her.

Marissa glared at him but stopped moving.

"Now. Would you like to discuss this like adults or do you need to go over my knee?"

Despite the shiver of excitement the threat sent through her, she shook her head. "*That* is not going to happen again."

Gage leaned down until their lips were only centimetres apart. "Oh, I believe it is. I believe it's just not in you to behave."

Trying not to let his proximity cloud her mind, Marissa closed her eyes and tried to be reasonable. She took a deep breath before speaking again. "Gage. You don't understand."

He frowned as he looked down at her. "About what exactly?"

"Do you know what we just did?" Her voice rose and Marissa hated that.

"I have a pretty good idea." He rubbed intimately against her, showing her that he still had life in him yet. "Do *you* need a reminder?"

The electricity between the two of them was so hot Marissa was surprised her hair wasn't on fire.

He bent and licked her from collarbone to ear. "Have you forgotten already?"

"Oh...I..." She didn't get any farther when his mouth covered hers. With her wrists still bound in one of his hands, she was helpless to push him away or bring him closer. She was able to wrap her legs around his waist. He rubbed against her swollen wet opening as he seduced her mouth.

"No, you don't need a reminder, do you? You remember just fine," he said softly. Then, with his gaze holding hers, he entered her slowly.

Marissa thrust her hips up, taking him completely. "More."

"Yes, more." Gage kept his pace slow and deep. Releasing her hands, he cupped her hips to hold them, not allowing her to set the pace.

"More. More."

Almost pulling completely out before slamming back in, he gave her what she needed. "This isn't something you can just ignore, Marissa."

"Just...protecting...you..." She spoke between pants as he picked up speed.

Gage raised her legs over his shoulders, taking him deeper with the next thrust. "I'm...the...Alpha." He gritted his teeth to keep from coming before her.

Her muscles gripped and massaged him each time he entered her. She was so wet, allowing him to easily pump in and out, but the fit was tight and felt better than any women he had ever been with. It was almost as if her body had been made for him.

When normally that thought would have sent him running, with Marissa, he found himself getting lost in the thought.

As Gage slammed into her harder, Marissa cried out. Her climax came quick and hard, making her arch, taking him in further. She milked him with her body, feeling like velvet around him. Releasing inside her, Gage shook as his seed poured into her.

Chapter Four

"Marissa..." Gage didn't know what to say to express his feelings. To tell her that she was his.

Reaching up, she cupped his cheek and his heart twisted in happiness at her intimate gesture. "I'm not trying to be difficult here, but by being with me..."

Gage caught a familiar scent and stiffened as his head snapped up. Now was not the time for visitors.

"What?" Marissa pushed at his chest.

Standing, Gage pulled Marissa up with him. "Someone's coming."

"Who?" She went in search for her clothes once again. Her shirt was right beside where she'd been laying. She blushed as she picked it up.

"I know who it is and they are deliberately making enough noise so we hear them."

"So they know we're here?"

Turning around, Gage kissed her forehead. "Your shorts are tangled in the tree root."

He watched as she pulled her shorts and shirt on quickly. She looked over at him, and he didn't miss the look of hunger in her eyes as she looked at him still without his clothes. Then she looked towards his clothes in a silent message. Gage wasn't in any hurry to put them back on and wished she hadn't been either.

"Gage."

"You have a great body."

"Gage. Someone is coming," she whispered with a look of horror on her face.

"They're already here." Turning, he faced his second-in-command.

Logan kept his head down and his smile hidden as he faced his Alpha. It wasn't the first time he'd seen him naked as they routinely ran together.

Now thinking more clearly, Gage was glad Marissa had covered herself up. He didn't want anyone else to see her.

"Alpha," Logan greeted, keeping his head down respectfully. Gage knew it was more for Marissa than him.

He crossed his arms over his chest. "Logan." Marissa had moved behind him even though she had pulled clothes on.

"I…uh…Elizabeth came home to have lunch with her sister and got worried when she wasn't in the house. She called up at the main house so I came over…to…uh."

"Oh God." Marissa dropped her forehead onto Gage's back.

Gage saw Logan unsuccessfully try to smother a laugh. "We'll be right up."

Nodding, Logan started to back away.

"Take the short way," Gage ordered.

Marissa kept her face hidden in Gage's back until he passed. "Oh God."

"Relax." Stepping away, Gage bent down and grabbed his jeans. "We're adults."

Her face was red and she kept her eyes on the ground. "I am so sorry. I didn't know she was coming home," she mumbled, but he heard her clearly.

Gage shrugged into what was left of his shirt. "Wouldn't have mattered. Once I saw you standing at the edge of the trees, I would have had you anyway."

She didn't respond to his announcement but turned away. "Have you seen my panties and bra?"

Recognising the change in subject, Gage decided to let it go for now. "Bra's by the tree, although I believe it's toast."

Marissa picked it up. "Panties?"

Gage pulled them out of his pocket. "They were under my pants."

Marissa held her hand out.

Gage just smiled at her and stuffed them back in his pocket.

"Gage."

"Come on." He reached out for her hand and pulled her towards the house.

"Gage, give them to me."

"No."

"Why do you want them? Some kind of trophy?"

Laughing, he continued to pull her. "Whatever you want to think, Marissa." He couldn't very well tell her that they smelled like her and he planned to carry them with him at all times he was away from her.

"Just don't see why you'd want to keep them," she complained but didn't say anything else.

Walking into the house, Marissa felt a new wave of embarrassment. Not only was her sister there but also the man from the woods and Elizabeth's mate.

Marissa tried to pull her hand away, but Gage tightened his grip.

"Marissa, I was worried when you weren't in the house and didn't leave a note. I'm sorry I..."

Again Marissa tried to pull her hand away but couldn't. "It's okay, Elizabeth," she tried to assure her sister.

How could she explain to her sister in a room full of strangers that the mistake was her own? She didn't want Elizabeth blaming herself. Marissa was the one to mess everything up. All she had to do was control herself and she couldn't even do that. Two days and she was already breaking laws.

"No. I shouldn't have called up to the main house..."

"Elizabeth, it's fine." Marissa waved a hand—unfortunately, it was the hand still holding her torn bra.

Elizabeth gasped as Logan and Greg laughed out loud.

Whipping her hand behind her back, Marissa pulled on the other one, and Gage finally released her. When she would have run upstairs, he put a firm arm around her waist and held her in place.

Marissa wished the floor would open and swallow her. But instead of making excuses about what had obviously happened, Gage just held her tight against him. Knowing he needed a way out and away from her, she tried to come up with anything she could to get rid of him.

"I need to take a shower," Marissa said to no one in particular. She was surprised when Gage smiled down at her and turned to the others.

"Gentlemen, why don't we leave the ladies to clean up and have lunch?"

Everyone agreed and the men headed for the door.

"I will see you later tonight, Marissa," he whispered in her ear before releasing her and walking away.

Marissa waited for the front door to close before lifting her head. Her sister stood with her arms crossed over her chest and the look of disapproval written all over her face.

"Don't," she warned Elizabeth.

"You didn't learn the first time?" Elizabeth asked, concern evident in her tone and by the softening of her expression.

"It was an accident."

"An accident?" her sister repeated with no amusement. "Tell me, just how do you accidentally get naked and have sex with the Pack Alpha?"

"How do you know I had sex with him?"

Elizabeth just lifted a brow.

"Okay, fine, I had sex with him!" Marissa started out the room.

"Why?" Elizabeth asked, following.

"It's not like I planned it." She couldn't explain it to her sister until she was able to explain it to herself yet.

"Marissa, he is my Alpha." Elizabeth's voice rose, and it reminded her of when they were kids and Marissa had once again gotten herself in some sort of trouble.

"I know."

"I can't believe you did this." The disappointment she heard doubled the guilt Marissa already felt.

Reaching the guestroom, she pushed the door open. "You know, he did have a say in the matter."

"Yes, he did." Elizabeth sighed. "I'm sorry, but you know what happened last time. This is my Pack, and that is my Alpha. I won't let you ruin that for me."

When Marissa turned, her eyes burned with tears. "I didn't mean to ruin anything."

Elizabeth's sigh was audible. "You know that male wolves for some reason think they are above the law. I'm sure Gage wasn't thinking about it at the time, but you should have."

Marissa *knew* she should have. "I'm sure he thought he would be able to keep it quiet. Brandon always told me not to tell anyone about us and I'm sure that's what Gage will tell me later."

"If this got out..." Elizabeth took a step back and had tears in her eyes.

"I'm sorry, Elizabeth." Marissa couldn't be any sorrier for her actions. Once again, she would be responsible for them losing everything.

Her sister sent her a sad smile. "Maybe it would be best if you left. Tonight."

"Okay." Turning towards the bathroom, Marissa felt the first tear fall. It *would* be best. For everyone concerned.

* * * *

"We have a problem," Logan walked into the Alpha's office without knocking.

"What?" Gage looked up from the papers in front of him.

"Greg just called. Elizabeth sent Marissa home."

"She what?" Gage's voice rose as he jumped up.

Logan took a step back. "After we left, Elizabeth sent Marissa back to California. She's probably already to the gate."

Yanking up the phone, Gage had to control his temper to keep from crushing the piece of plastic.

"Guard house," the guard on duty answered.

"Tom. Has Marissa Boyd driven through yet?"

"No, Alpha. No one's been through for about fifteen minutes, and that was Sammy and Kyle."

"She doesn't leave," Gage told him.

"But-"

"Don't let her out," he ordered. "I'm on my way." Slamming down the phone, he turned to Logan. "Get Elizabeth up here now."

Logan nodded and backed out of the room.

"What do you mean I can't leave?" Marissa banged her fist on the steering wheel. She shouldn't have been surprised. She'd known Gage wasn't finished with her.

He didn't understand that she had to leave. For both their sakes. She knew she should have said goodbye but had decided to take the coward's way out.

"Open the gate!" she ordered to the poor guard. It really wasn't his fault.

"I'm sorry, ma'am, but I have orders you are not to leave territory."

"I don't care what your orders are. I'm not a Pack member and you can't keep me here."

"I'm sorry, ma'am."

"Listen here, let me out!" she pleaded almost desperately. She had to get out of there. It was best for the Pack. They had to understand that.

"No, he won't."

Marissa jumped as Gage came around the side of the car. "What the hell are you doing here?" she asked, although she was afraid she knew.

Gage nodded to his guard, who looked relieved to be dismissed from dealing with her. "Where are you going?" Gage kept his voice low and calm. His eyes were hard as he looked at her.

She looked away from him. Guilt and shame kept her from meeting his gaze.

"I asked you where you were going," he said sharply.

Tightening her hands on the wheel, Marissa kept looking straight ahead. "Home."

Gage yanked the car door open. "Move over."

"No."

Reaching down and unbuckling her seat belt, he pushed her towards the passenger seat. She didn't have any choice but to move before he sat down in the driver's seat.

"Hey! Hey! You can't do this!" She grabbed at his wrists and hands.

Gage ignored her and put the car in reserve.

"Gage, stop!"

When the road was wide enough, he turned the car and headed back towards the houses.

"Gage, please stop." She didn't want to fight with him. She didn't want him to give her the lecture she knew was coming.

"Let me leave, please. On my own. I promise not to come back."

"Let you leave?" His voice rose. "Do you really think I'm just going to let you take off without a word?"

"This isn't about you, Gage. I...I just have to leave."

"No. You're not running, Marissa."

"She asked me to leave!"

Gage looked over at her as he navigated the road. "Because of me."

Marissa looked away.

"That's what I thought."

She sat quietly next to Gage. She didn't have anything more to say.

* * * *

Elizabeth sat with her hands in her lap, nervously rubbing them together. She hadn't expected Gage to take her sister's leaving well, but she hadn't expected to be ordered to his office.

She glared at her future mate who stood next to the bar talking quietly with Logan. Greg had called Logan when Elizabeth explained why Marissa had left. Greg hadn't been happy either. Didn't they understand she was trying to protect them and everyone in the Pack?

She jumped up when Gage walked in with her sister in tow.

"Sit," he snapped at Marissa, pointing to a chair.

Elizabeth saw her sister start to refuse until Gage turned those fierce grey eyes on her.

Marissa lowered herself into the wingback chair with her back to the window.

"Out," he ordered the two men.

Gage nodded at Elizabeth to sit. Once she was settled back on the couch, he sat behind his desk. Elizabeth tried to catch her sister's eyes but Marissa wouldn't look at her.

She really should have handled the situation better, but she was scared Gage wouldn't let her mate with Greg now. She'd almost lost her position once in a Pack because of her sister. Of course, that hadn't been Marissa's fault. She'd been young and in love, and Elizabeth couldn't blame her for what had been out of her control.

"Explain," Gage looked at her, speaking quietly.

Elizabeth ran her sweaty hands over her pants. "I believe it best if Marissa leaves."

"Because of what happened earlier between her and me?"

"She doesn't belong in Pack territory." Her heart almost broke at the sound of Marissa's breath catching. She didn't want to hurt her sister, but she didn't have much of a choice.

"Yet you asked permission for me to let her come. Now you want her to go?"

"Well, I didn't know... I mean, I..."

Gage nodded before looking at Marissa. "How do you feel?"

Marissa's face was blank and her eyes had turned cold. It was an expression Elizabeth hadn't seen on her sister's face since she left their former Pack.

"I was leaving, wasn't I?" Marissa told him, her face and tone not giving away any feelings.

"Just like that?" Gage continued to speak calmly. When Marissa didn't answer him, he looked back at Elizabeth. "I'm beginning to think I have missed some important information about your old Pack."

"I told you everything, Alpha. I didn't hide anything!" This was it. He was going to kick her out. Tell her she can't mate with Greg.

Instead he looked back at Marissa. "In the woods, you said you were trying to protect me."

Marissa glared at him. "Yeah, so?"

"Protect me from what?"

She didn't answer. Elizabeth was used to her sister's attitude but could see Gage was losing patience. She opened her mouth to answer, but Gage cut his gaze to her and shook his head. Elizabeth closed her mouth and looked at her sister. Marissa still wouldn't look at her.

"And you will harm me, Marissa?" Gage asked as they both watched her sister.

Marissa only shrugged. Elizabeth wanted to come to her sister's defence, but knew she couldn't help her. It broke her heart that once again Marissa would be thrown out of Pack territory.

"Answer the question," Gage said louder, making Marissa press back into the chair.

"The law," she finally told him.

"What law?" Gage looked from Marissa to Elizabeth with a confused look.

Marissa crossed her arms over her chest in response.

Gage looked over at Elizabeth.

"The one against mating with a non-shifter," Elizabeth answered.

"The law against mating with a non-shifter," Gage repeated.

Marissa jumped up from her seat. "Can I leave now?"

"Sit down!" he snapped though he didn't raise his voice.

Elizabeth almost fell over in shock when her sister dropped back down in her chair.

"Who told you about this law?"

"Our Alpha," Elizabeth answered.

His gaze never left her sister's face. "And what did he tell you would happen?"

"Because she…she was…"

"Because I fucked his son not only could I be kicked out of the Pack but so could my entire family," Marissa exploded, jumping up and smashing her hand onto his desk. Elizabeth jumped, but Gage didn't show any reaction.

"And were you all?" Gage asked, even though he knew the answer.

"I agreed to leave and never return so my sister still had a Pack to protect her," Marissa answered, anger burning in her eyes.

He stood and came around the desk. She didn't step back but stood straight when he stepped in front of her.

"Marissa." He wanted to hold her. To comfort her.

"And I'm willing to go now so you don't have to kick her out. No one else needs to know. I'll leave quietly," she told him.

Gage gently cupped her cheek, but she jerked away from him. "I'm sorry for everything you have been through."

Marissa remained stiff so he turned back towards Elizabeth. "While it may have been that Pack's rule, it is in no way a law. I have never heard of anything more ridiculous."

"If that's true, then..." Elizabeth trailed off, and Gage knew she was piecing together that they had been lied to.

"It's true," he assured her, then looked back at Marissa. Reaching for her, he drew her to his side.

"Then Marissa didn't have to leave."

He watched the play of emotions on Marissa's face before her eyes chilled again and she pulled away. "You don't know what you are talking about." Her voice was barely above a whisper.

Gage shook his head. "Why do you think we have a council of former Alphas to police the Packs? It's to protect the members, not to hurt them." He could see Marissa started to shake in front of him. "My father is one of the council members and I can assure you that, whether you can shift or not, he would have never allowed you to be mistreated. There is no such law."

"It *is* a law!" Marissa yelled.

He knew she wasn't trying to convince him but had come to terms with it.

Her eyes started to swim with tears and Gage's heart broke for her.

"Oh, Marissa, I'm so sorry," Elizabeth moved towards her.

Marissa held up a hand to stop her. "Whatever. It doesn't matter."

Elizabeth looked at him and he nodded. "Go out and find Greg. We'll finish up here and I'll drive Marissa back to your house."

"Marissa has her own car. And it's already packed," Marissa interjected.

Gage didn't even look back at her but kept his gaze on her sister. "She'll be okay here with me."

"Okay...I'll...see you both later." Elizabeth quickly made her exit.

"Come here, baby," Gage said once his office door closed.

"I want to leave."

Gage closed the distance between them and wrapped his arms around her. "Yes. I think you do. But not yet," he told her gently.

"No." Marissa tried to pull away. "Now. I want to leave now."

"It's okay, baby." Gage held her tight as the tears she'd been fighting started to fall.

As she cried in his arms, anger swelled inside him at the Alpha who had pledged to take care of her then turned her out without a Pack, without her family.

Tears streaming down her face she looked up and him and pressed her lips to his in a desperate kiss. Glad to be able to take some of the pain away, he let her kiss him and tightened his hold around her.

Chapter Five

Marissa pressed herself against Gage. His body was strong, solid, and everything she needed right now.

Gage's arms tightened around her as he kissed her back. When he pulled away and looked at her, Marissa felt her heart skip. She could get used to this man being there for her. And that was scary.

"Upstairs. I want you in my bed," he whispered in her ear.

Marissa shivered at his declaration. No more hiding. No shame in being with a wolf. She didn't have to hold back her needs with him. "Okay, upstairs."

Gage took her mouth again, this time with more force. Marissa gave herself to him willingly. He lifted her off her feet easily and she wrapped her arms and legs around him.

"We'll also talk about your punishment for talking back to me. Again."

Marissa scraped her teeth over his neck. "Maybe later."

Gage chuckled. "Much later.

They barely made it up to his room without her ripping his clothes off. Luckily they didn't run into anyone to slow them down. Gage kicked his bedroom door closed as Marissa teased him with her tongue on his neck and ear.

When he dropped her carelessly onto the bed, Marissa bounced, laughing before she looked around the room. "Oh wow."

Gage already had his shirt over his head. "Yeah. Strip."

Ignoring him, Marissa knelt on the giant bed and took in the large room. "This room is huge."

Although there were no lights on, she could see clearly enough. The bed was up two steps on a platform. To her left were balcony doors and to her right a sitting area with couch, table and chairs, and a flat screen TV. A door on the far wall would probably lead to a bathroom.

"You're not undressed," Gage practically growled at her.

Marissa looked at him and took in the naked body in front of her. Lean and muscular. Tan with no tan lines. She made quick work of removing her clothes and scooted closer on her knees. "Your room distracted me. Now you have distracted me." She licked a small circle on his chest.

Gage pulled her back by her hair. "Strip for me."

Marissa pressed a kiss into his chest. "Please let me do this, Gage." She needed to feel in control. Since first arriving, she had felt like her life was spiralling around her and she was only a passenger.

His eyes softened, telling her he understood. "Okay, baby."

She reached out and pulled him onto the bed. He let her lay him on his back before she straddled his waist.

Marissa took her time kissing Gage's lips, running her teeth over his neck and chin, before lavishing his chest. Keeping his hands at his sides, he allowed her to explore his body. And what a body it was. She breathed in his scent. Rich, dark, and male. She rubbed her face and body against his as she moved down.

"Marissa." Gage tried to pull her back up, moving his hands into her hair, but she continued to lower herself to the object she wanted most. His gorgeous, fully erect cock. Licking from the base up, she felt him let out a rush of breath. Then with just the tip of her tongue, she teased the head.

"Marissa," Gage hissed out, raising his head to look down at her.

Oh, she could definitely get used to this. She opened and took him deep into her mouth. Gage groaned and dropped his head back down. Adding her hand, she stroked and sucked him deeper into the back of her throat. He was salty and her body responded as his hips bucked to press himself deeper into her mouth.

"That's it. Suck me, baby," he murmured to her approvingly.

Marissa did. Tipping her head back, she took him as far as she could while sucking him deep.

"Stop," he ordered.

She hummed and swallowed, trying to push him over the edge. To make him lose control like he always seemed to manage with her.

"Stop!"

Marissa gave him one last lick before looking up. He stared down at her. His eyes glowed, showing just how close she had been to making him lose control and spill into her mouth.

"Come here," he commanded, and she didn't see any reason not to get what she wanted—him deep inside her.

She moved up his body slowly, arousing both of them with the rub of her body on his. When she was straddling his thighs once more, he gripped her hips. Lifting herself, Marissa took Gage's hard cock in her hand and teased her pussy lips with it. Moaning, she continued to tease them both until he growled.

She took just the tip of him inside as she bit her bottom lip, trying to control her need. Sliding down slowly, she felt her body adjust to his girth. When he was fully inside, she rocked forward.

Gage moaned, or maybe it was her—she couldn't tell anymore. He felt so good filling her. As if he was the only one who belonged there. Still gripping her, he began to thrust up to meet her every time she rocked. Marissa cried out, throwing her head back. She rode him faster as his hips lifted to meet her. Gage matched her speed, pulling her down harder each time.

"Yes." Marissa leaned forward, her hair streaming over both of them, making a curtain around them.

She was almost there. That sweet release was only a few strokes from taking her. They moved in a rhythm that built in intensity, but it wasn't enough.

Slipping one arm around her waist, he flipped her onto her back. He must have felt the need for more, too, because he slammed and pounded into her harder.

"Oh, oh," Marissa panted out. She was there, ready to explode.

"Stay with me," Gage grunted out, plunging inside incredibly fast and hard.

Marissa felt her body spasm. Reaching up, she grabbed his arms. "Yes. Harder."

Roaring as if his control was gone, he took her not only as a man takes a woman but also as a wolf would take his mate. She was still screaming when the first orgasm passed and another hit stronger, taking all her breath away. Gage threw his head back and yelled out his own release before collapsing on top of her.

* * * *

The day of the ceremony was busy for both Elizabeth and Marissa. Marissa took extra time to help her sister get ready — drawing her sister a hot scented bath, fixing her hair and make-up before helping her dress.

"That dress is beautiful. *You* are beautiful," Marissa told her sister, trying to hold back the tears.

"I can't believe it's finally here. I'm going to perform the mating ceremony."

Marissa leaned over and kissed her sister's cheek. "Not if you don't hurry."

Laughing, Elizabeth twirled around. "I'm ready."

Taking her hand, Marissa smiled. "Then I better get you there."

As she started to lead her from the room, Elizabeth pulled her back. "I'm sorry," she said quietly.

"There's nothing to be sorry about," Marissa assured, and meant it.

Elizabeth stood in front of her, and Marissa knew that regardless of how long she had avoided this talk, it was going to happen now. Or her sister wouldn't go.

"I love you," Marissa started, going with honesty. "I will admit that over the years I've been jealous of you. I didn't want to be different. I wanted to be either a were or a human."

"Oh, honey."

Marissa shook her head, cutting off Elizabeth's sympathy. "No. It's not your fault and it's not mine. Talking with Gage and Logan, I realised we both had a bad deal. We both deserved a better Pack than what we got."

"If I would have known…"

Marissa hugged her and then cupped her cheek. "But you didn't. Please, I want to give you this day. I want everything to be perfect for you. I'm okay."

"But…"

"I'm okay, Elizabeth. Please believe me."

"Okay." Elizabeth took a deep breath and Marissa was glad her sister hadn't cried. They didn't have time to fix her make-up. They were already late.

"So, let's go!" Marissa ushered towards the door.

Elizabeth smiled but didn't move. "One more question."

She knew what was coming. Even knowing didn't help with the answer.

"What about you and Gage?"

"I don't know."

"But you do care about him."

"I do," she admitted. "But I'm not a Pack member. I don't belong here. I have to go home soon."

"You could stay. Be part of the Pack. We could be close again." Elizabeth spoke of everything Marissa had already thought about.

"I can't. I'm sorry, but I just can't," Marissa told her softly. "Please don't let this ruin your day."

Elizabeth smiled but it didn't reach her eyes. "No. I won't let anything ruin today. I just wish you'd think about staying."

"What if I promise to visit more?"

Finally Elizabeth's smile reached her eyes and lit up her face. "Are you going to be coming to see me or Gage?" she teased.

Gage paced his office while Logan sat back comfortably on the couch.

"Nervous?"

"Of course I'm not nervous," Gage growled.

"She sure is something."

"Yes, she is. Everyone loves Elizabeth."

"I wasn't talking about her."

Gage stopped in front of him, noting the smug look Logan had. "What?"

"Have you talked to Marissa about staying longer?"

Gage went back to pacing. He'd tried to talk to her about Pack life. After all, committing to the Pack wasn't committing to him. But she changed the subject every time he brought it up. She was due to leave the next day. Every time they were alone together, he broached the subject. And she successfully distracted him.

"So you're just going to let her go?" Logan shook his head.

Gage knew he was only trying to help. There was a reason Logan was his second. The Pack respected him because he was fair, and Logan was like a dog with a bone. Never giving up on something he believed in.

"Maybe you don't deserve her then if you're just going to let her go."

"Watch your step, Logan," Gage warned.

"Excuse me, Alpha, but you are more than just my leader. You're my friend. I haven't seen you this relaxed...this happy in years," Logan pleaded. "And we both know it's because of her."

Gage walked across the room to stare out the window. He knew it was true. Marissa gave enough of herself to be intriguing yet held back, making her a challenge. She would spend time with him every night—sharing her body with him—yet she insisted on returning to her sister's house to sleep. She kept a distance between them and he wasn't sure how to push the issue without sending her running.

"It would be a mistake to let her go. Not only does she need a Pack to protect her, but you're in love with her." The last was said quietly, but to Gage's ears, it might have well been yelled.

Gage spun around, denial on the tip of his tongue. Then he felt the change in the house, in him. Elizabeth and Marissa had arrived. "They're here."

Logan nodded. "So let's get started."

They greeted the two women outside the door. Marissa smiled up at him and Gage felt his heart swell. He *was* in love with her. Even if it had only been a week, even if he hadn't told her yet. The wolf inside him had chosen her and the man couldn't have picked better. But Gage knew she would be harder to convince.

"Hi," Marissa greeted, looking beautiful in her short summer dress.

"Hello." Gage leaned down and kissed her mouth. The blush that stole her face would have been cute if it didn't tell him what he already knew. She was okay with what they did in private, but publicly, she still shied away.

"I...um..." She nervously shifted from foot to foot. "Thanks for doing this."

Gage nodded and hugged her to his side. "You can thank me later," he whispered into her ear.

She gasped, and Elizabeth and Logan laughed out loud.

"Most of the guests have arrived and Greg is already outside," Logan, ever the peacemaker, announced.

The look of relief that crossed Marissa's face was comical. "She's ready," she responded, avoiding everyone's eyes.

Gage laughed, letting go of Marissa. He knew he shouldn't tease her in front of others, but now that he had admitted to himself that he was in love with her, he wanted to shout it from rooftops.

But first, he had a ceremony to perform.

"You look beautiful. Greg is very lucky," he told Elizabeth, kissing the top of her head.

"No. No. I'm the lucky one. I know that. He has been so patient with me for all these years." Elizabeth took a deep breath. "I love him."

"I know you do, honey. And it's time to do this." Marissa hugged her sister.

Logan offered Marissa his arm. "Allow me to take you to your seat, my lady."

Shyly Marissa put her arm through Logan's. She liked him. He'd never treated her differently even after the embarrassing scene in the woods.

Logan led her out the back door to where the ceremony would take place. Gage would follow when it was time for the ceremony, escorting Elizabeth. As they headed to where the chairs had been set up, Marissa looked around, taking in the full picture. White lace and ribbons had been hung up. Her sister and Greg would stand under the arch while Gage performed the ceremony.

Light-hearted, Marissa smiled at the guests and Logan escorted her to the front.

She felt the unsettling sensation of eyes on her before understanding who stared at her. Turning her head, she met the pair of dark brown eyes, eyes she knew so well. Eyes that had haunted her dreams for more years than she wanted to remember.

Almost stumbling in surprise, she was glad Logan was there.

"What's wrong?" he whispered.

"Nothing," she lied. He would know it was a lie. Not only could he smell it, but also she had started to tremble. She didn't know what Brandon was doing there but it couldn't be good. She watched Logan look over also and knew she wouldn't have a choice in telling Gage.

"Who is he?"

Tearing her gaze from Brandon's, Marissa held onto Logan. "My old Alpha's son," she whispered.

Logan got her to their seats in the front row. He would sit next to her for the ceremony—that had already been decided. She was now grateful for the arrangement as she could feel the other man's eyes on them as they sat.

When the music started, announcing Gage and Elizabeth, Logan placed his arm around the back of Marissa's chair. She tried to relax as she concentrated on her sister.

The ceremony was beautiful, and watching her sister commit to Greg brought tears to Marissa's eyes. It also served to take her attention away from the other guests. She watched Gage as he stood with pride and presented Greg and Elizabeth to the Pack and guests.

When his eyes met hers, Marissa felt a shiver of excitement through her entire body. He was like no other man she'd ever met. While he was domineering and demanding, he still remained calm and kind. She would have never thought that all the traits he carried could be found in one man, a wolf, and a Pack Alpha.

She felt Logan's arm nudge her, reminding her it was time to stand and walk to the reception. Marissa purposely kept her gaze straight ahead, avoiding any guests. She didn't know why Brandon was here and she should have no fear from him now, but years of fear were hard to just replace. The promises and threats he'd made were still fresh in her mind.

Logan led Marissa to her sister, and as they hugged, he motioned for Gage to step aside. Marissa held her sister, then Greg took her in his arms and kissed the top of her head.

"I always wanted a sister. My mother had eight boys."

Laughing through happy tears, Marissa tilted her head back. "Well, you got one now. You have no idea what you're in for."

Also laughing, Greg kissed her cheek. "I'll hold you to that, Marissa."

Marissa understood the warning. She wasn't done with this Pack. Greg considered her family and wouldn't let her disappear out of Elizabeth's and his lives.

"What is it?" Gage asked, never taking his eyes off Marissa as he saw tears sparkle in her eyes. He knew she was thrilled for her sister, but he just wanted to hold her.

"I believe we have an unwanted guest," Logan kept his voice low so only his Alpha would hear.

Gage watched Greg kiss Marissa's cheek in a brotherly gesture. "Who?" he asked, distracted.

"Marissa's ex. The Alpha's son."

Shock had him giving his full attention to Logan. "Where? What did she say?"

"She was upset, although she tried to hide it."

"Find out what he's doing here," Gage ordered.

Logan nodded as they turned back towards the happy couple and Marissa in time to see a man place his hand on Marissa's back.

Marissa turned and stepped out of his reach. "Brandon," she greeted but her eyes remained cold.

"You look beautiful, Marissa." He placed a kiss on her cheek before he turned and shook hands with Greg. "Congratulations."

"Thank you." Greg looked between the new man and Marissa, knowing something wasn't right but unsure what to do.

"Congratulations, little wolf." Brandon also kissed Elizabeth's cheek.

"Thank you." Elizabeth's voice was soft. She sent her sister a panicked look. "Wh…what are you doing here, Brandon?"

"I escorted my cousin."

Gage had seen enough and moved in beside Marissa.

"Gage." Her eyes pleaded with him as he stepped up to the small group.

She didn't want a scene, Gage recognised that. He was also the Alpha, and if anything happened his Pack would step in and that would be a mess.

The man turned to him. "Alpha." He nodded in respect. "That was a wonderful ceremony. One of the best I've ever witnessed."

Gage smiled and nodded back to the man before running his hand over Marissa's back and settled his arm around her waist.

He saw her flush, but she didn't move away from him. The other male's eyes narrowed slightly.

"Uh...Gage, this is Brandon. He is the son of the Pack Alpha where we grew up." Marissa shifted like she wanted to move away from him, but Gage tightened his grip.

"Nice to meet you." Gage didn't move.

"Actually I am now the Pack Alpha of the territory. My father has retired," Brandon said, keeping his eyes on her.

Gage kept calm. That announcement changed things. If Brandon was a Pack Alpha, he couldn't challenge him without permission from the council that policed the Packs.

"Congratulations then," Gage told him with no feeling.

Marissa looked from one man to the other. Gage knew she was almost desperate to get away from Brandon. They would have to talk about what happened between the two later, but right now his main objective was to help her out of her distress.

"They're starting the reception. We should take our seats." Gage told her sliding his hand to hers. "If you'll excuse us," he said to Brandon but didn't wait for a response.

He walked away taking Marissa with him while Greg and Elizabeth followed.

"I get the feeling I missed something," Greg murmured to his mate, but Marissa and Gage heard him.

"That man is responsible for almost every problem we had in our old Pack." Elizabeth's voice held more bitterness than Gage had ever heard from her.

Marissa shrugged a shoulder and tried to pull away from Gage. He didn't give. He could still feel the other man's gaze on them.

Seated between Gage and Logan, Marissa pulled at her hand once more. "Let go, Gage," she complained so low only he could hear.

He was hanging on by a thin shred of control. His heart raced and his blood boiled in anger towards Brandon for everything Marissa had gone through. Plus suspicion as to what he was even doing here.

He looked over at Logan and could see the same feelings were going through his second. Whether Marissa was part of the Pack or not, she belonged to Gage.

He had never been so close to turning because of loss of control in front of any members of his Pack. He looked around and nodded at the Pack Enforcers. It was their job to protect their Alpha. Each one was keeping a close eye of their leader, sensing something was not right.

Marissa scooted her chair closer to him. Under the table, she placed her free hand on his knee. "Look at me, Gage," she whispered next into his ear.

He did and she smiled.

"I'm okay. I won't let anything mess tonight up."

Not caring who was looking, Gage framed her face with both hands. "Neither will I."

Marissa dropped her gaze. "Please, Gage."

She wasn't comfortable with public displays. He understood that even if he didn't like it. He dropped his hands from her face. "He's not to get near you alone. Do you understand?"

Marissa nodded even if it galled her to have him give her orders.

"Marissa." His voice was a low growl.

"I understand," she told him quietly.

"Make sure, Marissa. You have no idea of the consequences," he warned.

"I promise, Gage."

With that, he relaxed next to her.

Chapter Six

Marissa intended on keeping her promise. She didn't want trouble for anyone. She didn't know why Brandon would even come to her sister's mating ceremony, but he couldn't touch her. She told herself that over and over again.

The seating placed her with Gage and Logan while members of her and Elizabeth's old Pack took up two tables across the yard. The other tables were filled with Gage's Pack. Everyone was behaving properly, but one wrong move from either Alpha could spell disaster. Wolves were territorial about almost everything, but particularly about their women. She didn't want a Pack war at her sister's ceremony.

Gage or Logan stayed with her the entire time. After pictures were taken, dinner served and cake cut, the dancing began. Marissa danced with Gage, then Logan, but her attention was never too far from the man in the back keeping his eyes on her.

Walking to get a refill of champagne, she stopped to talk to a few of the females who had openly befriended her from Gage's Pack. If they knew she was a non-shifter, it didn't seem to bother them. Logan was talking to two of the Enforcers, but kept an eye on her from a short distance.

Marissa received her refill and turned from the table, running into Brandon. She tried to step around him, but he moved also. She looked for Gage or Logan, but they were several feet away from her involved in conversations.

Sighing, Marissa pulled her shoulders back and met Brandon's gaze. "What do you want?" she snapped.

Brandon stepped towards her. "Interesting seeing you interact with another Pack."

Marissa dropped her eyes out of habit, her confidence leaving her as he spoke with authority.

Satisfied, he moved even closer. "We have a lot to talk about."

"We have nothing to talk about," she said to her feet.

"Oh, you are very wrong. As Alpha of the Pack, I now have access to all the data on you and your family."

"So?"

"So as your Pack Alpha—"

"You are *not* my Pack Alpha," she interrupted.

Lifting his hand, he brushed her hair off her face. "Actually I am."

"I was kicked out of the Pack. You have no power over me."

"Well, funny thing about that. My father never turned in your papers to the council to let them know you were leaving the Pack. As law states, a member cannot leave the Pack and go rogue without a trial or the proper paperwork. You still belong to the Pack. To me."

"No." Marissa stepped back, shaking her head. She wouldn't go back to his Pack. She'd die before ever returning to him and giving him power of her once again.

Brandon laughed. "Yes, it's true. And by Wolf law, I have full control over you for your safety and wellbeing."

"You don't know anything about laws. You are a liar just like your father."

Anger flashed in his eyes and Marissa felt true fear. Her throat went dry while her heart pounded. Reaching out, he grabbed her arm. Marissa frantically looked around for Gage or Logan, not seeing either.

"No one's going to come to your rescue this time." He yanked her to him.

Marissa could feel his breath against her cheek.

"And be careful of your words. I will not let you disrespect my father."

"Let me go!" Marissa desperately tried to pull away from him, the need to run and hide almost overbearing.

"Or what?" Brandon ran his cheek over her hair. "You are mine. And you will be coming back to the territory with me."

Tears filled Marissa's eyes. This wasn't happening. This couldn't be. "No."

"What? Don't want to leave your lovers?" He spat at her. "Just how many of the wolves here have you spread your legs for?"

Marissa shook her head and again tried to pull away.

"I already know you are fucking the Alpha and his Beta. Is it just those two or did you take them all?"

As he shook her, Marissa's head snapped back painfully. They heard a growl before she was knocked away from him. Looking up from where she'd fallen on the ground, she saw a blur of movement as two males went down on the ground.

It took a moment for Marissa to recognise the man fighting with Brandon as one of Gage's guards.

"Stop!" she yelled to the two men. They didn't hear her…or choose to ignore her.

It wasn't until there was a second growl and Gage ordered, "Stop" that all movement ceased around her.

Marissa looked up to see his furious eyes boring into her. The muscle in his cheek jumped as he clenched his teeth. Marissa immediately dropped her eyes.

"Sam, go to my office," he told his guard, keeping his voice even, not giving away what he was thinking.

Sam picked himself off the ground, looking one last time at the man he'd taken down. "Yes, Alpha."

"Marissa, come here," he ordered next.

Marissa moved quickly to obey. Wrapping his hand around her wrist, Gage held her next to him. Logan stepped into the middle of the group and nodded at his Alpha.

"I believe our guests have overstayed their welcome. Now that the couple has left, they shall be escorted out." Gage's voice was low and deadly. Daring anyone to challenge him.

"I'll see to it, Alpha." Logan nodded and reached for Brandon, who pushed his hands away.

Standing on his own, Brandon faced off with Gage. "I agree we should be leaving. We'll just be taking Marissa with us," he said smugly.

Marissa stepped behind Gage, using him as a shield. She wasn't going with Brandon. She didn't think Gage would make her, but if what Brandon said were true, he might not have a choice.

"I don't think so." Gage didn't sound amused as Brandon stood in front of him.

Brandon smiled. "As her Pack Alpha, I will be returning her home."

"Pack Alpha?" Gage looked over his shoulder at her. Marissa shook her head. "I think not."

"She was born into my Pack."

"And left your Pack at the request of your Alpha."

"Really?" Brandon challenged, crossing his arms over his chest. "I have no paperwork supporting that."

"Of course not." Gage nodded as if he understood.

Marissa panicked. "Gage."

"Hush," he ordered. "Well, then I suppose you have the paperwork stating that she does belong to your Pack."

The smile faded on Brandon's face. "I do. Not with me though."

Gage shook his head. "I cannot in good conscience turn over a female who I don't know truly belongs with you."

Brandon took one step forward. "You would start a war over this slut?"

Marissa gripped the back of Gage's shirt. She didn't think Gage would turn her over to the other man, but doubt still made her stomach tighten with nerves.

Gage didn't move but met the other Alpha's stare. "Would *you*? You are in my territory now."

Brandon relaxed his stance. "We'll see about this." He turned and walked away, his Pack members following him.

"Make sure they all leave, Logan. Then I want you in my office."

Logan nodded first to his Alpha and then to the other Enforcers who had surrounded them. They all left silently.

Turning, Gage grabbed Marissa's arm and pulled her towards the house.

"Party's over," he threw back over his shoulder at the other members of his Pack, having them disperse quickly.

Marissa remained quiet as Gage led her away. In the shoes she wore, she kept tripping. Gage didn't slow his steps, however, he just tightened his hold. Marissa didn't fight, scared and unsure of her future and what Gage would do.

Sam jumped up when Gage walked into his office with Marissa. Gage pointed to the couch and waited for Marissa to sit before turning to his Enforcer.

"I apologise for my action, Alpha. I have no excuse for starting a fight with another wolf without your permission."

Gage nodded. "Yes. Especially another Alpha."

Sam's eyes widened. "I can only say that I was protecting the woman that my Alpha had taken as his own."

"And for that I thank you. Stand down, Sam, you are not in trouble."

Sam relaxed. "Is everything okay?"

Gage shook his head and walked behind his desk. "I don't know. But I have a favour to ask."

"Anything, Alpha," Sam agreed without second thought.

"We have a problem with the other Pack. Marissa will be staying here at the main house. I would like for you to go to Elizabeth's house and bring Marissa's belongings here."

Gage saw Marissa open her mouth and then close it quickly.

"Then we are on high alert. I want a full watch. Especially around the house."

Sam nodded. Logan knocked and entered the office. Gage acknowledged him with a tilt of his head.

"Then I would like you stay here at the house with Logan and I, in case there is any trouble."

"Of course, Alpha."

Gage dismissed Sam and turned to Logan.

"They're gone. The gate is closed and locked. I have four men on guard there," Logan informed him.

"Good. Make sure Sam has the others doing rounds." Gage told him even though he knew Logan would take all the precautions that were needed. Still he felt better knowing everything would be in order to protect Marissa.

"Yes, Alpha. No one will get in without permission."

Gage wanted more security than that. "I want no one else leaving."

"I'll make sure of it," Logan promised and Gage knew he would be taking care of things personally.

Gage looked over at Marissa. She had been silent the entire time. "Get me what you can, Logan."

He didn't need to tell Logan more for his friend to understand that he wanted everything on Brandon and the other Pack. Logan glanced at Marissa before he nodded and silently left the office.

Gage walked to Marissa and wasn't surprised when she leaned away from him. Now was the time for comfort.

"Come here," he said.

Slowly Marissa stood and took his hand, keeping her eyes down at her feet. Gage gently led her from his office and up the stairs. Once they reached his bedroom, he let her enter first. Marissa walked into the large room and sat on the edge of the bed.

Dropping to his knees in front of her, Gage gripped her hands. "Marissa."

Marissa didn't hold back her tears any longer. "I'm sorry, Gage! I'm so sorry."

Getting up and sitting next to her, he wrapped his arms around her. It broke his heart to see her so upset. "Shh."

"I...I...don't know what to do!"

Gage held her close to him and tried to make her feel protected. "I'll take care of it. Take care of you," he promised her and meant every word.

"He'll start a war. I don't know why. But I know he will," she managed to get out between sobs.

"Shh. Baby, let him try," Gage told her as he stroked her back.

"I don't want anyone hurt because of me. I don't understand why he's doing this."

Picking her up, Gage took her to the head of the bed and pulled the covers down. He placed her gently down. "Please don't worry, Marissa. I will take care of this."

Tears still streaked down her face. "I won't go with him."

"I know, baby. I wouldn't let you even if you wanted to." Gage wiped the tears from her face before bending down and kissing her cheeks, nose, eyes, forehead before placing a light one of her lips.

"Sleep now. I'll be here when you wake." Gage waited until her eyes closed before he stood and thought about what to do next.

* * * *

Gage stood from where he sat at the table in his room. True to his word, he worked up here instead of his office. He studied the papers he'd gotten when he'd first looked into Marissa. Logan and Sam were in his office trying to find something else — anything else.

A phone call to another Alpha — Lamont from three territories away — had helped. He had even offered to send his best Enforcer and son Cain down if Gage needed any help.

Grateful to have the older Alpha behind him, Gage relaxed. As Lamont had stated, there had always been something wrong with Marissa's original Pack. And while they would probably find papers to claim Marissa as theirs, Gage could turn around and file a claim that Marissa had been thrown out and had not been protected by her Pack. Gage knew he had a good case for that. Marissa had been on her own for the past ten years.

It also meant that Gage would have to take her into his Pack to file those papers and keep her from Brandon. He didn't mind having her there. She'd be a good member, but he wanted more. He wanted a commitment from her. He'd found his life-mate.

The light knock on the door took his attention from his thoughts. Walking quietly to the door, he opened it to Hannah, one of the older females who helped with his house. She had worked for his father before him and had always been a surrogate mother to him.

"I brought you both some bread and soup. And made her some tea," she told him.

Gage opened the door wider to let her come in with the tray. She placed the tray on the clean side of the table before looking up at him. Hannah had been with the Pack for fifteen years. She had come to his father after a member in her old Pack had assaulted her. Her Alpha hadn't done anything and Hannah had run away. Gage's father had gladly taken her into his Pack and his home. She had cooked for the wolves and kept his house ever since.

"You're doing a good thing," she said, and Gage could see tears in her eyes.

Gage shrugged at the admiration in her eyes. "I'm not only doing it for her."

"I know." She placed one hand on his cheek. "She wouldn't make it there. It would take everything out of her until she slowly died."

Gage placed his hand over hers, sharing comfort with her. "I will protect her. Even if it costs me my life."

"I know." She smiled sadly. "And that is why I choose to follow you like I did your father." She left him with that.

Gage walked over to Marissa. She was curled up and had dried tears on her face. Running his fingers over her cheek, he watched her blink awake.

"Hi," he greeted once her eyes opened.

She blushed and looked away. "Hi."

Leaning over her, he took her lips. Marissa opened for him before wrapping her arms around his neck. Gage moaned into the kiss and pressed her back into the bed. The power and control she held shimmered beneath the surface. She pulled at his shirt, finally getting it over his head. Reaching up, she ran her tongue over his chest. The muscles under her mouth quivered and his breath brushed against her cheek.

Gage used his lips on her shoulders, then pulled the straps of her dress down her arms. She still wore the dress from the ceremony and he wanted it off her. Reaching behind her, he unzipped it, baring her to him.

The rest of the clothes were quickly removed as they touched and kissed each other's skin. When he positioned himself over her, he held her legs open with his own. As he entered her slowly, they watched each other.

Marissa lifted her hips up to allow Gage to slip in smoothly all the way. He filled her, and she started to move under him. Gage kept his strokes slow and deep, watching the emotions in her eyes as he brought her pleasure. Her mouth opened and small sounds came from her. Gage grunted as the natural pace picked up, his body demanding he take her, the wolf demanding he claim her.

Crying out, Marissa wrapped her legs around his waist, taking him deeper. "Yes. Gage Oh yes."

"Mine," he growled. "Mine."

"Yes." Marissa eyes glowed, showing the rare glimpse of her wolf. "Yes, Gage, take me."

Gage slammed into her over and over. "More. I want more."

"Yes," she cried out.

"Tell me you're mine. Mine."

"Yes. I'm yours. Take me Gage. Claim me." The words came out, flowed from her without hesitation.

That was all Gage needed to hear. He pulled out and turned her over. He placed her on all fours and entered her quickly, going all the way to her womb.

Gage thrust into her fast and hard. He slammed into her, holding her hips, his mouth running over her back. When he felt her body start to tremble and she cried out her release, he opened his mouth. His canines lengthened, and he bit down, sinking his teeth into her shoulder. Her blood filled his mouth and he claimed her as his own.

Licking at the wound, he cleaned it as he found his own release, pulling her along with him one more time.

Empty and satisfied, he turned her back over and took her mouth. He shared her blood with her, licking the inside of her mouth before biting down on his tongue, filling his mouth with his own blood. He held the back of her head firmly as he forced his blood into her mouth.

With the claiming and blood exchange finished, they collapsed as mates.

Chapter Seven

Gage held Marissa in his arms and caressed her body. She hadn't said anything since they'd finished the claiming, but she hadn't pulled away either. Her body remained relaxed and soft against him.

When she rubbed against him, he felt the wetness between her thighs—evidence of the claiming and mating still running through her body. Cupping her round curvy bottom, he lifted her up and onto his thighs.

"Ride me, baby. Fuck me."

She did. Moving up on her knees, she took him inside. She rode him fast, lifting herself up and down, her clit rubbing against him while he played with her nipples.

"Mine." He lifted his mouth to take one pert nub inside.

Marissa cried out, riding him faster, taking them both to a fast but powerful climax. Sweating and panting, she fell on his chest.

Gage held her tight. "I love you."

Marissa jerked and brought her head up. "What?"

Gage laughed at the expression on her face. With a hand in her hair, he brought her mouth inches from his. "You heard me."

"But—"

Gage nipped her lip. "I've claimed you. Why would I do that if I didn't love you?"

"To protect me. To keep me in your Pack."

Gage's stomach dropped. Was that what she really thought? Was that why she did it, allowed him to claim her? Gage started to move her off of him.

Marissa tightened her legs, holding Gage under her. Inside her.

"Marissa."

Marissa just shook her head. "I'm sorry."

Gage sighed. He'd been stupid. Thinking she would fall in love as fast as he had. But he'd known the first time he saw her looking defiant and angry that she was the one who would take his heart.

Using his strength, he lifted her off of him. She growled but he ignored her and stood.

"Where are you going?" she asked.

Gage didn't even turn around. "To shower. We still have a lot to do to take care of your old Pack."

Marissa watched his back as he walked into the bathroom and slammed the door. Well, that hadn't gone well. The wolf inside her complained and demanded she go after her mate.

She knew she should have told him that she loved him too. And she did. The first time he kissed her, he had taken her heart along with her soul. He was everything to her, but giving him knowledge of that was hard for an independent woman.

Huffing out an irritated breath, Marissa stood and walked to the bathroom. She smiled when the knob turned in her hand and she opened the door. She could see Gage, through the glass, with both hands braced against the wall and his head bent under the spray. Pulling in all her courage, she opened the glass door and stepped silently behind him.

He jumped as she touched his back. "What are you doing?"

Marissa leaned into him, pressing her naked body against his. "Helping you shower." She reached over and picked up the soap from the dish.

Using shaking hands, afraid of rejection, she began washing his body. Running her soapy hands over his shoulders, down his strong back, to the sculpted ass she wanted to sink her teeth into, she took in his scent. Mixed with sweat, soap, and her own.

Kneeling behind him, she began to run her hands up and down his legs. She slipped her hands over his body and massaged the flesh as she washed.

When she massaged his cheeks then ran a finger between them, his body shivered. Marissa liked the reaction. Gage had introduced her to so much in the past week. Maybe, just maybe, she could do the same for him. To show him how she felt.

She wasn't a hundred percent sure what she was doing. Her hand worked on its own as she washed and touched him. Her fingers found themselves between his legs, running over his anus before slipping forward to massage his sac.

He shuddered at her touch and she moved with more confidence. While massaging his sac and then his thick cock, she used her other hand to run over his tight hole. Slowly and carefully, she slipped just the tip of her finger carefully in and out.

His breath rushed out and he groaned. His hands on the shower wall started to shake. Marissa continued to stroke him with one hand while she pushed her finger into the back entrance that had never been penetrated.

His hips moved as she grew in confidence and fingered the prostate. If what she'd read in books was right, he would enjoy this. She knew he'd never had it done before—they'd talked about all their sexual experiences and likes. He'd told her this was something he was willing to try with the right partner. And *she* was the right partner, the only one he would have from now on, and she was a mate who wouldn't share.

She matched her rhythm on his shaft, the strokes in and out of his ass, finally pushing her finger all the way inside. His hips moved forward, rubbing against her hands before slamming back against her finger. Gage picked up the speed with his movements and Marissa added a second finger. He groaned and she knew he was close to climax. The hoarse cry that tore out of his throat echoed around the bathroom as his body bucked and he started to spill his seed over Marissa's hand and the shower tile.

Once he'd released, Marissa took her hands from him and started to kiss her way up. When she reached his shoulder, she bit into it. Gage's body jerked under her. When she slipped between him and the shower wall, she met his eyes.

"I love you Gage. I have from the beginning. And you are mine too."

Emotions broke out over his face, and he wrapped his arms around her and kissed her all over her face.

He ignored the light knock on the door. When the knock came again, he lifted his head and yelled. "Go away!"

The knock sounded again and they heard Logan's voice. "I apologise for interrupting Alpha."

"Then don't," Gage complained, keeping contact with her.

"Yes, sir. I wouldn't, except we have a visitor that has arrived."

Gage's face shut down before he reached over and turned off the water. Grabbing a towel, he wrapped it around his waist before looking back at her with hot, promising eyes. He handed her a large towel before yanking the door open.

"And just who did you let in without my permission?"

"Your father, Alpha."

Marissa's heart sank.

Gage laughed, surprising her. "I should have guessed. We'll be right down."

"Yes, Alpha." Logan stepped away from the door and Gage beckoned for Marissa to leave the bathroom with him.

Gage pulled his clothes on quickly while watching her do the same.

"I hate to see you cover that beautiful body," Gage teased.

Pulling on her jeans, Marissa sent him a dirty look. "Well, I'm not meeting your father without clothes on."

Gage stalked towards her. "Okay, how about just without the panties?"

Marissa moved out of his reach. He could have caught her, but he was trying to relax her. It was obvious she was nervous about his father being there. "Come on! It's your house now too."

"Absolutely not! It's bad enough we both have wet hair so he'll probably guess what we were doing!"

"Oh he'll more than guess since we smell like each other and sex." Gage wrapped an arm around her waist as she tried to pull her shirt on.

"Stop that!" Marissa ordered, but he didn't miss the smile playing at the corner of her lips.

Once she was dressed, he held out his hand. "Then let's go get this over with then so we can get back to what we were doing."

Marissa put her hand in his and he pulled her from the room.

"What's he doing here?"

"He probably heard about the trouble."

They walked into the living room just as Logan handed Gage's father a glass filled with brown liquid.

"Father," Gage greeted.

The man stood and walked over quickly. "Son."

The two men stood for a moment before laughing and embracing in a big hug. The embrace lasted several minutes before the older man turned his eyes to her. Stepping away from his son, he took in Marissa.

She looked practically ready to run. Gage knew his father would understand and put her at ease. Even before any of this happened, Gage had told his father about her.

"You must be Marissa."

Marissa nodded and dropped her eyes. Gage wanted to tell her that wasn't necessary, but his father moved first.

"My daughter," he said softly as he hugged her to him. "I welcome you into my family."

When he pulled away, Gage noticed the surprise on her face and knew his father hadn't missed it either.

"I am so pleased to meet my son's chosen."

Marissa glanced over at Gage, and he smiled at her reassuringly. She relaxed visibly and looked at his father.

"It is nice to meet you too." Her voice was soft but strong. Showing her strength even when she was afraid.

His father took her arm and headed for the couch. Gage followed and sat in a chair across from them. Logan remained by the door, still on watch.

"We'll have plenty of time to get to know each other better, but first, let's discuss this situation with the other Pack," his father told Marissa as they sat.

Thirty minutes later, Marissa was arguing with both men.

"There should be no challenge!" Her voice rose above the rest.

Gage shook his head. "He will challenge me. And I have to accept." He knew she didn't want him to, but she had to understand where he was coming from. Protecting her was his duty.

"You don't have to do anything," she argued.

"He must protect his mate." His father spoke the words Gage had been thinking.

Frustrated, Marissa stomped to the window and looked out. "I don't want anyone getting hurt because of me," she said more quietly.

Gage wrapped his arms around her, and rested his chin on the top of her head.

"Baby, even if we weren't mated, which we are, I would accept a challenge from him for everything he put you and your sister through." He turned her around so he could look in her eyes. "I love you. I will make sure you are always protected."

Reaching up, Marissa cupped his cheeks. "I love you."

As their lips met in a soft kiss, all of their troubles seemed to melt away. As the kiss went deeper, he heard someone clear their throat from across the room. They broke away, but Gage held onto her.

"Sorry," she mumbled, embarrassed.

Gage's father's eyes were bright with unshed tears. "It's understandable. I can remember—" His cell phone ringing cut him off.

The conversation was quick and brief. Marissa knew Gage could hear what was being said on both sides of the phone. Her hearing, while good, wasn't *that* good. When the phone call was over, Gage hugged her tightly.

"There will be no challenge," Gage's father announced.

Marissa relaxed. "Really?"

He nodded. "Seems Brandon's father stepped in and won't allow him to take this any further."

"Oh thank God!" Marissa kissed Gage quickly. "What's wrong?" she asked when he didn't say anything.

Gage smiled and kissed her back. "Nothing, baby. This is good. Why don't you go upstairs and change, and we'll take my father to town for a steak dinner?"

Marissa nodded even while she looked suspiciously at him. He knew she would still worry, but he didn't want her involved in the next discussion. She looked over her shoulder before she opened the door and he sent her what he hoped was a relaxed smile.

Gage waited until he heard the bedroom door open before speaking. He looked at his father and then his Beta.

"This isn't over. No matter what they say. They are up to something."

Logan took a few steps from his post by the door. "I saw his face when he said Marissa belonged with him. It doesn't matter what his father told him."

Gage's father rubbed a hand over his face. "I agree with both of you. And since he is Alpha now, he doesn't have to follow what his father says."

Gage thought of when Marissa had told him that she loved him. He hadn't cared about the other Pack. He'd only cared about having her in his arms for the rest of his life. He wasn't about to give that up.

"From everything I've read and what Marissa's told me, I don't think he'll come at me through proper channels."

"An ambush, maybe?" Logan suggested.

"Or they may just try to take her," Gage's dad mused out loud.

"They won't get her," Gage assured the men. "They would have to get through me first."

His dad nodded, but worry was etched on his face. "That doesn't mean that they won't try."

"Let them. I would love a chance to go after that entire Pack for what they did to Marissa." He fisted his hands in anger just thinking about what his mate had gone through. He slowly unclenched them and ran a frustrated hand over his face.

"You need to keep a calm head," his father advised, walking over to refill his glass.

"And what would you do?" Getting angry, Gage began to pace the room.

His father took his time refilling his drink and took a sip before responding. "I'm no longer the Alpha of the Pack, so it doesn't matter. What does is how you handle this threat to your Pack."

Gage took a deep breath before speaking. His father had always run the Pack fairly, and they'd thrived under his leadership. "I understand I can't go looking for trouble. But if they bring it to me, I will be ready for them. The only way they'll get to her is to come into my territory."

Logan cleared his throat and drew both men's attention. "So she's not leaving?"

"Of course not!" Gage shouted.

Logan nodded and dropped his eyes in a submissive gesture.

"Damn! I'm sorry, Logan. I didn't mean to take it out on you."

His father walked over and threw his arm around Gage's shoulder. "I think I'll take a rain check on dinner. Logan can keep me company. You need to go see your mate."

Gage went without looking at either man. Who would have thought falling in love and claiming a mate would make him feel so out of control?

Chapter Eight

"Would you like to repeat that?" Marissa asked even though she was certain she heard Gage correctly.

"You need to make arrangements to have your stuff sent here," he told her.

He currently prowled the bedroom floor, looking very much on the edge. He had been sweet and loving last night, and that morning when he'd woken her in the most pleasurable way. Now, fifteen minutes later, he was issuing orders.

"My stuff?" Marissa kept herself calm, knowing one of them had to be. "I think we need to discuss this."

"What's to discuss? You are my mate. I can't leave my Pack or my territory, so you have to move here," he announced, looking at her like it didn't even need to be said.

Marissa took in his demeanour and knew this could turn bad, real fast. "Gage. I don't know that I want to live on Pack territory."

She saw the change in him immediately. His eyes went flat and cold, and his face hardened.

"You don't have a choice."

"I...I don't have a choice?" Her voice rose and she knew she was just as close to losing control.

"That's what I said. *You are my mate!*" he yelled.

"I may be your mate, but I don't belong to you, Gage Wolf!" she yelled back. Forget being calm. She wasn't going to let him dictate to her about her future.

"Actually, that is *exactly* what that means!"

Gage watched as Marissa's face fell and she jerked as if he'd just struck her. Damn, this was not going the way he wanted. He hadn't meant to bring it up at all, but he just wanted her safe in his home, in his arms.

"I didn't mean it like that," he said and took deep breaths to relax himself.

She turned away from him and he had to stop himself from reaching for her.

"I think it is what you meant, Gage. You may not be like my old Pack Leader, but you are an Alpha."

"I am in no way like your last Pack Leader. This Pack is nothing like your old one. The sooner you realise that the better off you will be."

"Maybe," she said softly, turning back towards him.

He could see unshed tears and it broke his heart that he'd hurt her. "Baby, I'm sorry..."

She held up a hand to stop him from approaching. "I know I have issues, Gage. You knew that coming into this. I can't just forget everything in my past. And you can't expect me to drop my entire life."

"You actually think that you can just walk away from me, from your mate? Marissa, think about this."

"I am. What happens ten years from now when I become too much trouble? Hell, it could happen in one year."

Ignoring the fact that she didn't want him to touch her, Gage embraced her. "That won't happen."

She tilted her head back and her eyes met his. "You don't know that." She moved from his arms. "I'm going for a walk, alone," she told him as she started out of the room.

"Marissa." Gage stopped her with words even though he wanted to use force. "Don't—"

She sighed and interrupted him. "I won't leave the territory, but I wasn't asking for permission."

Gage watched her walk away. The woman who had stolen his heart and held it in her hands. He would love her forever. He could feel it and the wolf inside him agreed. He knew he needed to be patient with her, that she had a lot to get past, but he needed her to start making her way to him. To his Pack. He needed her with him. It was more than just sexual. He needed her like he'd never needed another person.

And he wasn't certain he could suppress that need for long.

Marissa walked the woods behind Gage's house. The farther she got, the more peaceful she felt. It was only yesterday that her life had changed. She had seen her old lover, taken a mate, and committed herself.

She had no intention of leaving. She knew her place was here with Gage. It was the Pack she still wasn't so certain about. No matter how hard she tried, she couldn't help but compare them to the one she grew up in. As happy as she wanted to be, there was something in her head telling her that it wouldn't last.

Marissa walked farther into the woods until she reached the creek that ran through the middle of the property. She sat at the edge and stared into the water. It rippled and flowed past her as she let her eyes close and felt herself drift.

It was beautiful here. Even though she couldn't shift and run like the others, she could still feel at peace. She could be happy here, with Gage, with her sister. She was so tired of being alone. For the first time in her life, she had more than just her sister. She had a future, a chance, and an opportunity to have a family. Did she really want to chance walking away from that?

A sound behind her had her opening her eyes and jumping to her feet. Marissa took in her surroundings, not seeing anything at first. When there was movement to her left, she turned and narrowed her eyes.

A man stepped out from between the trees and she tensed. He waved and Marissa recognised the guard from the first day. She'd seen him a couple of times since and he had always friendly.

"Steve," she greeted after he walked to her.

"Sorry, didn't mean to startle you," he said as he smiled at her.

"No. No it's okay. I guess I was lost in my own world."

"I could tell. You didn't even hear us approach."

"Us?" she asked, looking behind him.

"Us." His voice was joined by several growls. Three wolves stalked towards her as Steve opened his arms as if in a welcome. "Meet my friends."

Marissa backed as far as she could without falling into the creek. Steve and the wolves crept closer, and Marissa frantically tried to find a way out. The wolves snapped and growled at her.

"What's going on, Steve?" Marissa asked.

"It's nothing personal. I actually like you."

"Well, I don't think those wolves are the welcoming committee. Why are you doing this?" she demanded.

"Because I paid him."

Marissa was so surprised when Brandon stepped from the trees Steve had come from she almost stumbled into the water.

Brandon laughed once she had righted herself. "Easy there, Marissa. Don't want you falling in now."

"Wh…what are you doing here?"

"Did you really think this was over? That you were done with me?" He took a step towards her. "I decide when we are finished."

"You already did. If I recall, you decided and then I was run out of the Pack," Marissa reminded him.

"Yes, well, I changed my mind. Who knew that you would turn out to be such a hottie? Or that you would fall in love with another Alpha?"

Realisation hit Marissa. "That's what this is all about." She glared at Brandon. "You don't want me, you just don't want anyone else to have me."

Brandon looked amused. His lips turned up and his eyes were shining. "Well, aren't you just a little conceited bitch?"

"Maybe, but I know I'm right." She looked from him to the wolves. "So what's your plan here?"

"It's simple. You come with me quietly or I'll have the wolves tear you apart. After they are done with you, I will send them to your mate, and then your sister, and anyone else I think you care for."

"You wouldn't…"

He smiled again and flashed his canines at her. "Oh, I would. I would."

"All right. I'll go with you." Marissa could only hope that someone would see her and stop Brandon from taking her.

Marissa walked from the creek in the direction of the house, being careful not to get too close to Brandon. The wolves followed behind her.

Brandon let her pass between him and Steve. Marissa held her breath.

"Not that way." He grabbed her arm and yanked her to him.

"What?"

"Not that way." Brandon started walking and pulled Marissa along with him.

She tried to dig her heels in, but her strength was no match to his. He easily dragged her as he walked in the opposite direction of the house. Away from Gage. No one would see them if they continued to head this way.

"Wait! What about my stuff?" Marissa tried to stall.

"Don't worry, you won't need anything," he assured her.

"What are you going to do with me?" Marissa could feel the tears fall. She couldn't go back with him. She had to trust Gage could protect himself, to watch over her sister. She just couldn't go with Brandon.

"Whatever I want," he said as he continued to take her farther away.

Desperate, Marissa did the only thing she could. She screamed as loud as she could. She didn't stop even as Brandon turned, pulled back his fist, and punched her.

"I told you to be quiet," he yelled as he struck her again, knocking her off her feet.

Marissa wasn't going to be quiet. Screaming was the only way to let Gage know she was in trouble.

"Shut up!"

With a hit to the side of her head, Marissa felt her vision blur. She put her hands in front of her, trying to ward off the blows.

Brandon stopped hitting her but remained on top of her. "I should have known better. You never did listen."

Marissa struggled, but didn't have much fight left in her. "Get off of me."

"I don't think so." He ran his hands over her body. "I should get to have a little fun with you before I feed you to the wolves."

Marissa didn't have the strength to stop him when his hand found its way under her shirt. Her stomach turned at the feel of his hands on her skin, but she wasn't dead yet and she would fight him with her last breath.

"I think you'll enjoy it too. Remember how good it was between us. How hot it was."

Marissa shook her head. "No. It wasn't that great. I've had better human lovers. And you don't even come close to Gage."

"You little bitch," Brandon spat as he wrapped his hands around her neck. As he squeezed, Marissa tried to grab his arms.

"You need to get out of here." Steve's voice barely reached her from somewhere to her right. "Someone would have heard her scream. You have to leave before they come."

"It's too late for that." Gage's voice was the last thing Marissa heard before she passed out.

Gage had been standing on his back porch with Logan, drinking a beer and staring into the woods when he heard Marissa's scream.

He didn't remember jumping off the porch or running to her. He didn't hear Logan behind him or Sam and the other guards change into wolf form.

He just ran to his mate.

He reached her and saw Brandon on top of her with his hands around her neck. She fought him like the true solider she was. Taunting him with words when her strength wasn't enough. Hearing his guard Steve's voice warn the other man barely registered.

Brandon's head snapped up and their eyes met. The other man looked at him defiantly, but Gage could also see the fear. It wasn't enough for him. He wanted the other man's hands off his mate.

"Let her go, *now!*" he ordered in a low calm voice.

Brandon looked down one last time before removing his hands from Marissa's neck. He stood and faced off with Gage.

"What are you going to do?" Brandon asked smugly, but his gaze flickered around.

Gage could see Logan standing by Steve and his guards that were in wolf form had surrounded Brandon's wolves. The other Alpha was alone.

"Only what you deserve," Gage told him.

Brandon attacked. It was the opening Gage needed.

Both men changed in midair, coming down in wolf form biting and fighting. Gage easily got the upper hand and had Brandon by the throat.

Brandon's hind legs beat at his stomach, but Gage held on tightly with his teeth. He could taste Brandon's blood gush into his mouth and it tasted like heavenly victory. He shook his head, tearing the vulnerable throat even more.

This was the one that had caused Marissa so much pain. The man who had put the fear and distrust into her eyes. He would rip out his throat for doing it to any female, but the fact that he did it to Gage's mate made him want to savour the moment.

That's when Gage felt the touch to his own neck and Marissa's sweet voice next to his ear.

"That's enough, Gage." She stroked his fur. "He's not worth it. Let him go and face the council."

Gage growled, voicing his displeasure at her suggestion.

"Come on, baby. It will be more humiliating for him to have to face everyone than you killing him. He tried to take me against my will, he lost a fight with you, he will be finished as Alpha. As well as being in any Pack."

Marissa continued to stroke his neck and legs. Brandon had gone limp. Gage dropped the other wolf whose head landed on the hard ground with a loud bang. He was unconscious but alive.

Gage nuzzled Marissa and she wrapped her arms around him.

"It's okay," she whispered to him. "I'm okay."

Chapter Nine

Marissa ran between the trees, zigzagging and crossing her scent. The wolf chasing her was so close she could practically feel his warm breath on her. She jumped over a fallen log and changed directions, heading to the creek.

When the water came into view, she used the last of her energy and raced towards it. Before reaching it, she was knocked to the ground as the wolf's large bulk hit her. Marissa rolled as she fell and ended up on her back. Her breath came out in pants from the long, hard run.

The wolf stood over her, licking her face.

"Stop, Gage! Stop!" She pushed him away, laughing.

He gave a fake growl and settled down beside her. She closed her eyes and breathed in the sweet air.

It had been two weeks since Brandon had found her at the creek. She went back to this spot often but never alone. Brandon would stand trial, but his Pack was still out there. Steve had his trial last week and had been announced rogue. It was the worst punishment for a wolf other in death. He would not have a Pack to protect him and was literally alone. Gage had told her Steve was too much of a coward to come after them, but he didn't want to take chances. She had agreed to Gage's request that she not take walks alone.

Sometimes Logan would accompany her, or her sister, or one of the females she had made friends with, but most of the time Gage did. With Steve's betrayal, Gage would only let a handful of people around her. In the past, it would have driven her crazy, but now it made her feel more cherished. She loved the times they were alone out here. When she had the Pack Alpha all to herself.

Gage licked her arm and she opened her eyes. He stood over her, and she swore he was smiling down at her.

"Change back," she ordered. Ready for some of the human fun they had come out here for. Her body already tingled with need for her mate.

As he changed back, Marissa couldn't take her eyes from him. She no longer looked away when he made the transformation. Gage had given her the feeling of belonging she had always wished for.

Once in human form, he collapsed on top of her, his erection digging into her hip. She giggled and rubbed against him.

"Is my little wolf hungry?" he asked, raising his body just a fraction from her.

Marissa grasped the base of his cock and stroked him. "Always. Always hungry for you," she admitted.

He thrust against her hand, showing her he felt the same way. "Well, then I should take care of that." He slammed his mouth over hers and pushed his tongue inside.

Marissa sucked on his tongue, drawing out a moan from him. With hands shaky with need, he pushed her knees up to her chest and positioned himself at her hot, wet entrance. Without breaking the kiss, he plunged inside, swallowing her cry.

Once again, showing her exactly where she belonged.

PACK
ENFORCER

Dedication

This book goes to everyone who loves the wolves —
thanks for the support.

Chapter One

Emily Black kicked her shoes off and watched as they flew across her living room. Godforsaken things. She hated shoes no matter what kind they were. At least the tennis shoes she wore to class were more comfortable than the heels her friends wore.

She kicked them under the coffee table as she passed and stripped off her shirt and jeans while heading into the bedroom for loose shorts and T-shirt. Once comfortable, she headed into the kitchen. The fridge, which she kept overstocked, was cool as she opened it. She grabbed a bottle of water and the Tupperware full of lasagne she had packed.

Heating it up in the microwave, she sat on the counter to wait for it with a fork in her hand. Many people would consider her behaviour weird or think that she hadn't eaten in hours. But, for her, it was just another day. She had eaten lunch only two hours ago, but a shifter burned a lot of energy and needed to eat large regular meals.

She, however, ate many small meals. Especially around the few people she called her friends. Even though the world had finally admitted there were Shifter or Were creatures out there, she didn't like to call attention to herself. No one at school knew about her. Of that she was pretty sure. To them, she was just a quiet girl who liked to study and keep to herself. She was pretty in a traditional way, but not a head-turner. She would leave being stunning and charming to those around her. She preferred to blend in and not draw attention to herself.

She could see her answering machine light blinking, indicating she had a message, but wasn't in any hurry to check. It was probably someone trying to sell her something. She didn't get many phone calls.

* * * *

Cain knocked on the door to his Alpha's study and waited for the grunt meaning to come in. He entered and remained silent as Lamont finished his phone call. If Lamont hadn't wanted the conversation overheard, he wouldn't have let Cain in. Werewolf hearing was better than any device you could buy.

Cain immediately recognised the young Were's voice on the other end of the line. She spoke softly to the Alpha of the Pack, although her tone showed frustration. Hearing her voice sent a shiver down Cain's spine and a jolt to his cock.

They all worried about the young Were women who were out of the Pack's territory. In all of the attacks that had recently taken place, the females were away from home, out of Pack territory. Showing why he was Alpha, Lamont was calling them home before Cain had thought of it.

"Have some bags packed when your ride gets there," Lamont said sternly into the phone.

Cain barely held back a smile when he heard the order.

"No, someone will be there to pick you up." He looked over at Cain. "It will be someone you recognise from the Pack. Do not leave with anyone else."

Lamont listened for a few more minutes before cutting her off. "No. You will stay in one of the cabins. It will be fully furnished for your arrival." He waited again. "You'll stay until we know what is going on and I tell you it's okay to go back." That was all Alpha speaking to one of his Pack. Cain knew how Lamont felt about Emily. How everyone felt.

Emily had been changed as a child, which was against every rule and law they had. Most children could not handle the stress of change. That was why it was forbidden. Too many children had died back in the settling days before his family had a Pack leader. It was Lamont's father who had forbidden the change of children or anyone who did not choose it. There were too many risks.

Someone could carry the Were DNA two ways— through birth or by being bitten. However, being bitten did not mean they would automatically change. They must carry the strain somewhere down their line.

Cain's brother, Tony, could explain it better. Tony was a natural born talker. He could smooth over anything or anybody. He was the face of the Pack. When the Packs had decided to come out in the open, to stop hiding from the world, there needed to be a recognised face. A face that people could see and not think of a monster. Cain was just glad it wasn't him. He would rather stay home in his Pack's territory, keeping watch and protecting his Alpha.

He turned his attention to the man who sat behind the desk. A man he respected more than anyone else.

"Emily Black," Lamont told him once he hung up the phone.

"She's coming home?" Cain asked even though he knew the answer.

Lamont nodded at him. "I want every female home and safe. Especially her."

Cain understood what Lamont was saying.

They had rescued her from the cage she had been put into after she had been changed—when the ones who had changed her couldn't handle her. She had been filthy and bruised from head to toe. Neglected and scared with no idea what was going on. She'd been twelve. Now, ten years later, she would be coming home to be kept safe once again.

"I want you to go get her and get her here safely," Lamont told him.

Cain just stared at his Alpha. "Me? You sure? Maybe Tony would be better," he suggested instead. It wasn't that he didn't agree. He did—she needed to return home. He knew it was for the best. But after years of fighting his attraction to her, Cain wasn't sure being closed in a moving vehicle together was a good idea.

Lamont just looked at his second-in-command and raised an eyebrow.

Cain cleared his throat. "Of course. I'll leave right away." He turned to walk out.

"Cain," Lamont called after him. He waited until Cain had turned around and met his gaze. "There's always been something there between you and Emily. Do you want to tell me about it?"

Cain shook his head. "I'm not sure I know what you're talking about."

Lamont stood and walked around the desk. "I'm not asking as your Alpha. I'm asking as your father. Is there something between you that I should worry about?"

Cain understood the question that wasn't asked. He was a dominant male. Emily was still scarred and young. It had been cute, as she'd grown up, the little crush she had on him. She would follow him around instead of playing dolls; she would practice fighting and manoeuvres as he'd taught others. It hadn't hurt anyone, and both he and his father had wanted her to be able to protect herself. Never to be a victim again. That was the promise the family had made her when they saved her. That no one would ever hurt her again.

So the lessons had started when she was seventeen. It was the longest year Cain could ever remember in his life. There had been something instantly attracting him to her. The first time he'd touched her to show her a throw, there had been a spark. He could still remember the moment. The widening of her eyes, the catch of her breath, and the feel of her skin under his hands. He had backed away immediately, but the damage had been done. The attraction had been noted.

But the big episode had come at the end of a year of working with her. She was eighteen by then, but still safe and off limits to him. He had made a promise to protect her, and he would—even from him. She had just thrown him, and he kicked the back of her knee, having her go down at the same time. He shifted to break her fall, and her body fell onto his. She didn't rush or scramble off him as she normally did.

Their eyes met, and there was that connection once again. Then her mouth was on his, moist and hesitant.

It was a feeling he would never forget. Her lips moving and caressing while her hand rubbed his chest. He'd rolled her onto her back, taking control of the kiss, deepening it, making it hard and rough. His hands slid under the tank top that she wore, and he rubbed her breasts, pulling at her nipples as he kissed her mouth. She moaned, and he felt that into the deepest core of his body. He was between her legs, hard as a rock and ready to plunge into her the moment he could pull her shorts off.

He stroked down from her breasts past her stomach to her hot core. He slipped his hand into her shorts and inside her panties, shimming his fingers against liquid heat. As he brushed his hand over her centre, she pressed against it, begging him to take her. And as she moaned and writhed under his touch, the kiss became brutal. When he dipped his finger inside, she exploded and rocked and screamed at the climax that tore through her body.

He shook the memory away. He hadn't handled that well. He had come to his senses at the last minute. He'd stopped before it was too late, sent her back to the house and avoided her from then on. After that, she'd begged and pleaded with Lamont to let her go away to college.

Neither Lamont nor Cain had wanted to let her go. Being in Pack territory almost guaranteed her safety. Lamont had held off as long as he could, kept her there for four years at the community college in two towns over.

Finally, he had to let her go. At twenty-two, she'd left to go to the closest university. They would still worry with her being outside the territory, but she had promised one thing.

If trouble came, if she got a call from the Alpha, she would return home.

The call came now, and Cain would be the one to pick her up.

She'd returned every summer and for holidays to spend her time off with the only family she had ever known or could remember. So they had been thrown together numerous times but had managed to avoid each other and talking about what happened.

Obviously, they hadn't avoided keeping everything from the Alpha. From his father.

"No, nothing." Cain shook his head.

Lamont didn't look convinced, but nodded. "Then go get our girl."

Cain turned and left to go get the one girl he could guarantee wouldn't be glad to see him.

Chapter Two

Emily glanced up at the knock on the door. She had been sitting on her couch with her packed bags at her feet. She was needed at home. She knew this day would come, when Lamont would want her to return.

The knock sounded again, and she smiled. Nothing like an impatient wolf at the door. She opened the door, smiling until she got a look at the dark, handsome man standing there.

Damn.

Cain looked wonderful. He was over six feet tall with dark hair and gold eyes. His hair was longer than she remembered and fell over his forehead. Her fingers twitched to push it back. He radiated strength as he leaned against the doorframe.

She noticed his eyes took her in the same way as she was him.

"Surprised?" he asked with a nasty twist of his lip.

She shouldn't have been. Fate loved to throw her curve balls. And if her dreams lately were any indication, she wasn't over this handsome, cocky wolf in front of her. It was going to be a long drive. She opened the door wider to allow him in. "I was expecting Tony."

"Well, you got me instead." Cain stepped into the small apartment.

With a deliberate ease he walked past her and sniffed the room.

"What are you doing?" she asked as her eyes narrowed.

She knew exactly what he was doing. He was scenting for other men. But she hadn't been 'dating' anyone recently, so there were no others scents in her apartment but hers.

He just smiled back at her.

"Ugh." She stomped over to her two bags and picked them up. "Fine, let's go."

Cain's eyes lit in amusement. Whenever they were together, she could feel the tension in the room and in her body. They brought out the absolute worst in each other.

It took Emily twenty minutes in the car to finally give in. Cain knew she would. She always made the first attempt to talk. This time was no difference.

"Why am I going back?"

"That's where you belong," Cain told her, tightening his hands on the wheel.

She snorted. "Says you, but Lamont wouldn't have called me back without a good reason."

Cain glanced over at the woman next to him. It had taken all the control he had not to grab her in his arms the moment she'd opened the door. She was everything he remembered, everything he dreamt of at night. He could swear her scent had wrapped him into a web when he'd first seen her. Same now as she looked up at him expecting the truth. Weighing his options, he decided to tell her as little as possible.

"There have been some attacks on female Weres outside Pack territory," he said gently.

When her eyes widened with horror, he reached over and patted her leg. "No one in our Pack. It's been four women so far, but Lamont wants to be careful. The latest one was from Christian's Pack."

"Who?"

He frowned, thinking he should have left this for Lamont. "Mindy."

She turned and looked out at the passing scenery. "What happened to her?"

He shook his head. "You don't need to know that."

She turned then to look at him. "Well, I think that since I was called home due to it being a danger to me, and the fact that a good friend was attacked only two territories over, I should have a good idea of what is going on. I'm a big girl, Cain, I don't need you to protect me."

He shook his head again. She might be a big girl, but he would always protect her. "If you want to hit up Lamont for that information, that's fine, but I'm not telling you." He took a deep breath. "And I'll always protect you whether you like it or not." They both knew he wasn't only talking about with this situation.

He reached over, turned the radio on and put both hands on the wheel.

Emily just stared at him. She'd been dismissed. Just like that, he thought he could tell her that they weren't going to talk about it and they weren't. Well, he had another thing coming. She'd tried, she told herself. She would have been nice and polite, but his attitude just stank. She switched the radio off.

"Listen to me, Cain." Surprised, he looked over at her. She kept her voice low. "I'm not a child any longer. You can't pat me on the head and send me to my room."

He cleared his throat. "I never did that."

She laughed. "Yes, you did. I made a pass at you, you turned me down. We are both adults, and I think it's time you stopped holding a grudge." She crossed her arms over her chest and turned her head to stare out the window again. There. She'd said what she had wanted to for years.

"What are you talking about?"

When she didn't say anything, he whipped the car to the shoulder and slammed on the brakes. She had to put her hands out in front of her to keep from hitting her head, and the seat belt tightened around her body.

"What the hell!" she cried out.

He undid his seatbelt and turned to face her. "I hate to tell you that you're wrong, but being that you are, I'll force myself. I crossed a line with you. I shouldn't have, and I apologise. If the only way to make sure it doesn't happen again is to stay away from you, then I will."

Emily noticed his eyes were practically glowing. It was past time for them to talk about this, but *now* was most definitely not the time. But she had to know why he thought that.

He reached behind him to pull the seat belt back on, but she stopped him with a hand on his arm.

"What line did you cross?" she asked gently.

He growled in the back of his throat. "You know damn well what I did."

She nodded, not moving her hand. "I know what you did, Cain, and I know what you didn't."

He tried to pull away, but she tightened her grip. She might not be as strong or as fast, but in the small confines of a car, he couldn't move enough to avoid her.

"You refused an eighteen-year-old girl who jumped on you, who had planned for months for the right moment. Maybe I made a mistake. I don't think I did, but I know you do. I was eighteen and infatuated with you, Cain. You were all I could think about. When you sent me back into the house, it broke my heart."

It was time for honesty. This had been going on with them for far too many years. "I'm still not sorry," she told him. "And you didn't do anything to be ashamed of. It was my doing. And," she added with a small smile, "I can't promise I wouldn't do it again if I went back. No one's ever kissed me like that again."

He shook his head, but she noticed his lips twitched in amusement. "You were a child."

She shook her head sadly. "I stopped being a child at twelve, Cain."

"That's no excuse," he told her.

She blew out a breath. She had tried. "Fine, Cain, punish yourself. Do what you want."

Chapter Three

The next morning, Emily had breakfast with Lamont, and he told her a little more about the assaults than Cain did. More, actually, than she thought she wanted to know.

After breakfast, Toby, the youngest of the Alpha's children, talked her into making chocolate chip cookies for him. Every six-year old's dream. One of the guards had come in right after she had started and kept her and Toby company while she baked.

That was where she was when Cain walked into the kitchen — bent over the counter passing a plate of fresh chocolate chip cookies to Toby.

"What's going on in here?" he asked, casually leaning against the door.

Emily turned and rewarded him with a brilliant smile. "Eating cookies. Want some?"

He looked over at the guard who had straightened from behind her. "What kind?" He walked over and took one. "Eric?"

Eric cleared his throat. "Yeah, well, I better get back outside. Thanks for the cookies, Emily."

She smiled at him. "No problem."

Cain stood close to her, and she could feel irritation radiating off of him. She was getting really tired of this. He hadn't said anything else after their short talk in the car. She hadn't wanted to press him further at the time, but she wanted things to be different this trip. Every time she returned home, there was always so much tension between them.

For once she would like a good visit, to go back to how things had been. If he didn't want her, he shouldn't have any problems with her being there. But the tension coming off him told her that he indeed have a problem with it, with her.

He took another bite then said, "Go play outside, Toby," while still looking at her.

Toby frowned at the loss of his milk and cookies. "But I don't wanna."

He did look at Toby then and had him scrambling up from his chair and out the sliding glass door. Emily watched him go, preparing herself for round two with Cain.

When the door finally slid into place, she whirled around. "What is your problem now, Cain?"

She was prepared for a fight, not for being lifted off her feet and his mouth on hers. She was so surprised her mouth opened in a gasp. He used that opening to slide his tongue in. It was rough and brutal and bruising. It was everything she wanted from him. He didn't release her immediately, and the kiss made her lose all sense of her surroundings.

She wrapped her arms around his neck and her legs around his waist. She could feel his hard length pressed up against her. It made her moan and tighten her legs around him. He left her mouth and continued kissing, nibbling her chin, her neck, her shoulder.

While he leaned against the counter, one arm around her waist, he held her as he slipped the other hand under her shirt. He ran his fingers over the soft silk of her bra before pushing it away and finding her skin. She wanted to scream at how good his hand and mouth felt on her. She wanted to drag him to the floor and demand he take her like she had wanted him to for years.

Then he was releasing her, sliding her back off the counter and turning her away from him. Stepping back, he put her hands on the counter and straightened her clothes. She looked back at him, confused, hungry, and hot.

"Cain."

He just shook his head and nodded to the kitchen door. Not a minute later, Tony walked in. Emily busied herself washing her hands, using the cold water to try to relieve the heat burning in her body.

When she turned around, Cain didn't even look at her as he ate the cookies, not quite pulling off the innocent look he was going for.

"Good God, are you two fighting again?" Tony said as he continued farther into the room. He walked over to the counter and popped a cookie in his mouth. "The emotions swirling around in this room are enough to strangle a man."

Cain growled and stuffed another cookie in Tony's mouth. "Is he ready?"

Chewing the cookie, Tony brushed crumbs off his shirt. "Yeah, he wants to meet in the living room hoping Christian will be more comfortable."

"Christian's here?" Emily asked.

Cain's eyes narrowed.

"Yeah, he just arrived with Adam and Kyle," Tony gladly told her, obviously noticing Cain's reaction as well.

"Tell them to find me before they leave, will you?"

Tony nodded and grabbed another cookie.

"I'll catch up. Give me a minute," Cain told his brother.

He waited until Tony had left and they could hear his footsteps going down the hall before he turned to her. "Stay away from Eric and Kyle."

"What?" He had caught her off guard once again. She was expecting another 'Emily, that was a mistake'.

"You heard me," he said in a dangerously low voice.

She placed her hand on her hips as her eyes narrowed. "Oh, I heard you all right. I just think you should reconsider the orders you give me."

He walked slowly to her, his eyes never leaving hers. "Really?" He smiled, and it wasn't a nice smile, but one of the cat before he caught and ate the mouse.

She tossed her head. She would not be intimidated by him. "Yes."

He leant in. "Okay how's this? You'd better stay away from Eric and Kyle and anyone else I say." His eyes flashed.

"No." She said it more bravely than she felt.

"No?"

"You're not my boss. I can talk to who I want." She tilted her chin up.

He laughed. He actually laughed at her.

"Hmm, interesting." He ran fingers lightly down her check and she shivered. "Actually, I am your boss, Emily. I am second-in-command in this Pack. A Pack where you are a member."

She pulled away. "That doesn't mean you can tell me who I can be friends with."

He'd stepped forward as she stepped back so he was actually closer to her than he had been. "You don't want to push me here, Emily. Not with this."

"You're jealous," she accused.

"No, not jealous. Cautious." He had moved his hands up her arm and fisted one hand in her hair. He pulled gently and had her lifting up on her toes. "Do what I say, Emily." Then he kissed her quick but hard and walked away.

She was still sputtering out a response when he turned before going out the door. "And, Emily, you don't want to see me jealous."

Everyone else was already in the formal living room when Cain arrived. His Alpha sat in one of the chairs next to Christian. Kyle, Adam, and Tony stood by the bar.

Tony smiled at him as he entered, and Cain wanted to take his frustration out on him. Emily knew better than to argue. Where had the submissive young Were gone? She was argumentative and hard-headed. He knew he couldn't keep his hands off her much longer, and he'd be damned if he was going to share her.

Kyle and Adam both walked over and shook his hand, and he couldn't help but be resentful of Kyle. He was the only Were that had been close to Emily's age. They had become fast friends, and back then, Cain had been happy for her.

Now looking at the young wolf with blond hair and charming smile, Cain had to squash every instinct he had to crush his hand while shaking it. But when he turned to the two Alphas, everything jumped back in place.

Especially his responsibilities and the reason for Emily's return in the first place.

The other Alpha looked tired and worn out. Cain walked over to him and held out his hand as Christian stood. Christian had been granted Alpha status and land by Cain's father. He'd only had his Pack about thirty years.

That was not long in Wolf time. He had taken a few wolves with him when he'd started out—his family and others who'd agreed to follow the new leader. Now, Christian had a girl who'd been attacked. A girl who hadn't been protected. For an Alpha to not be able to protect one of his Pack members, especially a young female, was the worst crime in the laws, and Christian was taking it hard.

Lamont got right to business, going over every detail they had learnt so far and sharing theories. It was a long information switch meeting, running over three hours. When Christian recounted what had happened to Mindy, his voice cracked. Adam went over and laid a hand on the shoulder of his Alpha, his father, but Christian shook it off. It was his burden alone to carry.

Everyone in the room except the Alphas stood and listened. They spoke no words and asked no questions. That is the way it was in a Pack—follow the Alpha, absolutely, with no questions asked.

It was decided that Cain would work with Adam, looking into the attacks and taking care of the problem when located.

Gage, another Pack Alpha, was also sending his second, Logan, to Christian's pack for added security.

Cain did not like the idea of having to leave his territory during this mess. To leave his Alpha—and yes, Emily—without his protection, but he would have to.

The meeting wrapped up, and Cain walked out with Adam. Kyle walked out with Christian. Cain met

Lamont's eyes and knew he was to go back in shortly. His meetings were not over for the day.

"We find this bastard, and he's mine," Adam said as he stopped a few yards from the waiting car.

Cain understood what Adam was saying and nodded.

Adam nodded back. "I have another favour to ask." He looked back at Kyle. Cain had a really bad feeling about this favour. "I am asking permission for Kyle to stay in your Pack's territory until his sister has her baby."

Kyle's sister, Alisha, had stayed with Lamont's Pack and later bonded with one of their males. They were expecting their first child.

Cain wanted to demand Kyle's return back to his own Pack, but he nodded, knowing he would want to be with his sister if he had one.

"Granted until this is over."

Adam shook his hand and nodded at Kyle. The relief that spread from the other man wrapped around Cain. He had done the right thing. Now, he just had to keep Kyle away from Emily. And it wasn't jealousy, he told himself. He was only looking out for her, like he always had. It was his job.

Later that evening, he called Emily and set up a time for her to meet with him in the gym.

"I want you to meet me at eight in the basement," he told her as soon as she answered.

"What for?" Her voice was cautious with a hint of annoyance.

He almost told her because he'd ordered her to, but he knew that wouldn't go over well. "You need to get back to training. We're not sure how long you will be here but while you are here, it won't hurt to work out.

Especially with all that is going on." He wasn't used to explaining himself, and he didn't like it.

She was so quiet on the other line he wasn't sure she was still there.

"I don't think..." she started.

"Eight o'clock, Emily," he ordered this time.

She blew out a breath and muttered something.

"I'll see you then." He hung up without another word from her. She'd be there.

Chapter Four

Emily arrived tired, annoyed, and mad as hell. Who the hell did he think he was? Demanding she be at the gym in the stupid morning before any sane person should be awake. This was her vacation! She should be able to sleep until at least noon. He had no right to order her around, and she was going to let him have it.

He was waiting on her, of course, standing in sweat pants and no shirt, curling weights. Her heart jumped and lust flowed through her entire body. This wasn't going to work well.

So she used her anger and led with that.

"Who the hell do you think you are ordering me here at the butt crack of dawn to train?" she asked him with her hands on her hips.

He smiled at her in the mirror but didn't turn around.

When he didn't answer, she took another step closer. "I'm telling you, Cain, you better stop ordering me around. I'm not going to put up with it."

He lifted an eyebrow at her. "You wouldn't have come if you didn't want to." She fisted her hands at her sides, and he laughed. "I forgot you're not a morning person." He put the weights down and finally turned to her. "Now, would you like to stretch before we get started?" he asked sweetly.

She switched strategies. "This is not a good idea, Cain."

Cain continued to smile as he wiped the sweat off his chest. She almost moaned with the need to lick it off.

"Are you not the one who keeps telling me we are both adults?" he asked.

She didn't respond. Just turned and stomped to the other side of the gym and started stretching.

He gave her fifteen minutes before walking over and nodding to the mats. She sighed, but walked over to them and stood in the middle.

"Okay." She raised her arms. "I'm here. Now what?"

He smiled and circled her. "I think we'll start with hand-to-hand. You've seemed to have a problem lately with your reflexes. "

"What?"

"You've been pretty easily grabbed and touched and…mmm…kissed," he taunted.

She lifted her chin. She was a fierce competitor, and he knew it. Insults and challenges were always the way to push at her.

"Well, don't worry. I'm wise to your tricks now so we won't have that problem again," she assured him.

He threw his head back and laughed. Then he shot a foot out at her knee and made her crumble. She fell, but rolled and was right back on her feet.

"I wasn't ready," she told him, then tried a kick of her own that he easily blocked.

That started the twenty-minute battle. She landed on her ass at least a dozen times but was always right back up. She even landed half a dozen blows, one knocking him back pretty good. She finally landed a perfect jab with a kick to the back of the knee, sending him down. She yelled and clapped right before he swept her feet from under her.

He was immediately on her, sitting on her legs and holding her arms over her head. "Celebrating before your enemy is all the way out is never a good idea, Emily. I taught you better than that."

They were both breathing hard, but she smiled. "Got you down."

He looked her over with a slow, hungry gaze. "Did you? Hmm. but it looks like I finished on top now, didn't I?"

She struggled for a brief moment as he shifted his body in between her legs while still holding her arms above her head.

"What a very interesting position you seem to be in." He leant close. "Almost helpless." He licked the side of her face.

Her breath washed out of her, and she trembled with need. "Cain," she warned.

He moved his mouth down and licked her from her collarbone to her ear. "Yes?"

She couldn't help it—she moaned. "Don't. Stop."

He laughed softly and licked her again, this time from her ear to under her chin. She lifted her chin to allow him access.

"Which is it? Don't, or stop, or don't stop." He pressed close and teased her lips with his tongue. "Come on, Emily. Get away. Take me down." With his free hand, he slid it down her body, teasing with light touches.

She moaned, arching her back. "Let go of my hands," she demanded, her voice heavy with need.

"Make me." He brushed his fingers through her clothing over her centre, just hard enough to have her biting her lip to keep from screaming. "Make me, Emily," he said again before he took her mouth in a rough kiss.

He used his teeth on her lips. She pushed up and, using his momentum from the kiss, was able to change positions briefly before she was on her back again.

"Mmm, good." He rocked against her, and she could feel his hard erection.

"Cain," she pleaded.

He looked her in the eye and smiled. "Oh, you'll beg before I'm done, make no mistake." He took her mouth again, and she already wanted to beg.

He released her only long enough to pull her shirt off. He had her hands caged once again in one hand before she knew she'd been released. She struggled against his hold, but he didn't seem to notice.

"I want to touch you. Let go of my hands, Cain," she said as he continued to kiss her from the collarbone down.

"Then get your hands loose," he told her.

She struggled again, pushing up, and only managed to rub herself against the hardest part of him. For just a moment, she saw spots. She wanted—no, *needed*—him so bad.

Then, with his one free hand on her sports bra, he pulled and ripped the material. The feeling the sound of the fabric ripping was too much for her. She did beg. "Please, oh God, please."

He licked one nipple and blew on it. "Not yet," he told her, taking the nipple in his mouth and sucking.

She screamed, but he didn't release her. He used his tongue and his teeth until she was sobbing out his name. Her body was on fire. Never had she ever been so turned on in her life. Each tug on her sensitive nub shot through her body.

"Almost there," he told her, sliding his body down to concentrate on her stomach.

He released her hands, but she kept them above her head until he used his teeth to pull her pants down. She moved quickly, pushed up and had him on his back. He let her have the position as she reached down and pulled his pants off. He wore nothing underneath, and she purred as she cupped him.

Then she was on her back again with his mouth on hers. He slipped a hand down and brushed a thumb over her swollen centre.

"Now, Cain. Now!" she demanded.

But his body slipped down hers as he held her legs apart and feasted.

"You have no idea how long I've wanted to taste you," he murmured.

She screamed when he stabbed his tongue inside, using his tongue to separate her folds, then penetrating inside. His thumb circled her clit. Her hips bucked, and she was scratching at his shoulders. Too much pleasure assaulted her. His tongue caused each sensitive nerve to dance.

"Cain." She cried out his name as her body tightened and exploded.

"Yes, say my name," he told her as he knelt between her legs. "Mine."

He pushed just the tip of his cock inside, then stopped. "Look at me, Emily."

When she opened her eyes, he pushed farther in. "Say it."

She nodded, tears streaming down her face. "Yes."

His hands held her up and in position. Their eyes held. "Scream my name now."

And she did at the first thrust.

Emily felt her body stretch to allow him entrance. Cain moved with long, deep strokes, picking up speed as he slammed into her.

Emily lifted her hips and matched each thrust, her body taking him deeper each time. She was slick, coating him as he pulled out and then pushed back in.

Watching him, she saw his eyes start to glow. She knew she was giving him pleasure. "More. Harder," she panted out.

He groaned but lifted her hips higher so he could plunge in faster, his hips snapping a fast rhythm. Emily felt her second release tear through her body.

She dug her nails into his sweat-laced skin as he reached orgasm.

Chapter Five

Cain rolled off of Emily, and they lay side by side on the mat, trying to catch their breath. He got his first and propped up on one elbow and looked down at her. Her eyes were closed, and she had a small smile playing on her lips. He leant down and kissed that smile gently.

"Emily."

"Uh huh," she answered without opening her eyes.

"Emily, look at me," he told her softly.

She opened her eyes, "Cain, if you tell me that was a mistake, I think I might kill you. No, I'm pretty sure I will."

He laughed softly and adjusted her where she could lay on him and still look at him. "No, I wasn't going to… I want you to… I mean…" He sighed and rubbed his hand over his face.

"What?"

"I want to go on a run with you. Tonight."

He watched the surprise then pleasure and, at last, uncertainty flicker in her eyes. He held her breath as he waited for her answer.

"Run?"

He nodded. It was a big step for him. Going for a run just the two of them was what mates, what bonded, did. It was intimate. He wanted her to understand that she belonged to him now. To run in their other forms, their wolves, was a sign of commitment.

"Just us?" Her voice was quiet.

Cain didn't know what to think about the amount of time she was taking to answer. A male could not force a female. The females in a Pack were protected above all else. If she said no, he had to back off, no matter what. He only nodded in answer to her question.

She leant in and whispered her answer against his lips, "Yes."

He let out the breath he wasn't aware he'd been holding. He kissed her gently, running his hand through her hair that had come loose from its holder, trying to make up for how rough he'd just been.

He couldn't stop touching her. He had fought his attraction for so long. Now, having her in his arms, he knew he would never let her go.

He deepened the kiss and felt her shudder. "If we don't get up now, we won't make it to tonight," he told her, pulling away. He stood and lifted her to her feet. His hand covered the bruises on her wrists where he had held her. He stroked them with his thumbs.

"Cain."

"I hurt you."

"No," she said, placing a hand on his check. "You didn't. And these will be gone in an hour."

He stepped back to let her dress before he had her on the mat again. He pulled his pants on and watched her slip into hers. She looked at the ripped sports bra then pulled her shirt on without it.

Her breasts stretched the material, and her nipples were hard. He groaned and rubbed his chest. She was going to kill him. He picked up her ruined bra and stuffed it in his pocket before taking her hand and leading her up the steps into the main house.

He didn't drop her hand when they went into the kitchen and saw Tony sitting at the counter with a bowl of cereal, but he stepped in front of her and blocked her from Tony's view.

Tony looked up and smiled. "Did you have a nice...workout?" he asked.

Cain felt Emily lean her forehead against his back, and he knew she was blushing. Every room in the house had extra soundproofing because they had such good ears, but you could hear enough.

That and Tony would be able to smell them on each other, along with other smells.

Cain cut him down with a look that said to be gone when he came back.

Tony just continued to smile at him. Then he sobered. "Adam called. I told him you were a little...busy and would call him back."

Emily's grip tightened on his hand, and Cain growled at his brother who just blinked innocently at him.

He pulled her from the kitchen, but turned back just before the door closed and mouthed, "You're dead," to his brother.

Emily didn't say anything as they walked through the house and out the front door. When they reached the car she used when she was there, he held open the door for her then leaned in and kissed her before she could get in. He had her trapped against the car and his body.

He had meant it as a soft, quick goodbye kiss, but it deepened as if on its own, and his arms caged her to his body. She kissed him back with the same amount of passion and need he gave her. His body hardened, and he lifted her off her feet and leaned her against the side of the car.

He quickly scanned the area for any others who may have been walking by or the guards making their rounds, but the area was clear for the moment. Not that it would be a big surprise to anyone to see a couple making out or even having sex.

But Cain wasn't about to let anyone but him see Emily. The fact that it was the first time he had that thought did not escape him. In the past, when he'd been with another female, he hadn't cared if anyone walked in while they were together.

Her legs were wrapped around his waist, and he was pressed against her. She moaned and rubbed herself on him.

"Cain," she whispered when he broke the kiss.

"I know, baby. I know." He tried to release her but the pulse between his legs only increased when she moaned again.

He cursed and hitched her higher around his waist. Kissing her, he walked over to the trees on the north end of the property. It would keep them hidden from the house or anyone who drove up. He would hear or sense anyone else.

He barely had her on the ground before she was tearing his pants down. He did the same to her and plunged into her as his mouth covered her scream.

* * * *

"What is wrong with us?" Emily asked from under him as they came back to the world.

He rolled off of her and shook his head.

She blushed, pulling her pants back on. Her hands were shaking. He reached over and grabbed them. Her eyes met his and he saw her confusion.

"Emily?

"We just did it in the middle of the yard. Anyone could have walked by." She sounded nervous, and he smiled to reassure her.

"It's not unusual." He pulled her up to her feet with him.

She frowned at him. "No, Cain. I mean, I've been...uh..." She looked around, as if what she wanted to say would be written somewhere. "With others, you know, and it's never been like that. Well, like either time really."

She pulled her hand away and wrapped her arms around her middle. He embraced her, hoping to give her comfort.

"Baby, you haven't been with a Were before, only human men. That's bound to be different. Plus I am very good if I say so myself. I've ruined you for all others, human or Were."

"Don't be cocky." She pushed him away, laughing. She started walking back to her car but stopped so abruptly he almost ran her over. "How do you know I've always been with humans?"

He froze. He couldn't very well tell her he knew about every one of the men she had been with. Checked them out when she started dating them and kept an eye out for any problems. So he told her the other truth.

"Because I put the word out if any wolf touched you I'd kill them," he told her as he put his hand on her back to push her forward.

But she dug her heels in. "You did what?" Her tone was the first warning. The narrowing of her eyes the second. And her fist smashed into his face.

His head snapped back, and he saw stars of a moment. When he recovered, he looked at her and saw her eyes wide with surprise.

"You deserved that." she told him as she started back for her car.

He shook his head again. It wasn't to clear the pain but the shock. She'd just almost taken his head off.

He smiled and ran to catch up with her. "That was a good hit."

She sent him a sidewise look.

"You're right, I probably deserved it." He walked around her and then backward in front of her. He felt young again. Happier than he had been in years.

"Stop, Cain."

"Stop what?" he asked innocently.

Emily reached her car, but he was still in front of her.

When he in to kiss her, she pushed him back.

"No way, or I'll never get home. You can wait until tonight."

He sent her a mournful look before tucking his hands in his pockets. And, of course, that's where her bra was.

"Get in the car while you can then," he warned her.

She laughed and went around the door he had left open. Before she could close it, he grabbed her chin and kissed her long and hard. Her eyes were unfocused when they separated.

"Drive safely," he told her as he shut the door. And he could swear he heard her growl.

Laughing, he headed upstairs to shower. He'd never felt so light-hearted in his entire life. He was already in his room with his pants off before he remembered he needed to kill his brother and call Adam back. So he made a mental note—shower, call Adam, and kill brother. That ought to do it, he laughed to himself.

* * * *

He never did go after Tony. The call from Adam changed that.

"Another girl was attacked."

"When, where, who?" He grabbed for a pair of jeans.

"Riker's territory in Colorado. He did the same as the other Alphas and called the Pack home. Girl was fourteen miles from territory."

"We need permission to go up and talk to Riker, and the girl." Cain was already making plans in his head.

"Done. Christian's already called. We leave at first light."

Cain nodded then said out loud, "Good. Good."

"Just me and you. Riker doesn't want anyone else around the girl."

Cain frowned into the phone. "It was bad?"

Adam sighed, and Cain could hear it clearly over the line. "Very. I'll be there to get you at six."

"I'll be ready," Cain promised, then went downstairs to give his dad the news. He didn't want to leave Emily. The fact that she was his first thought instead of the attacked girl confirmed that he was already in over his head. He had a job to do. Even if all he really wanted was to curl up in bed with Emily and shut out the world.

Chapter Six

Cain returned home tired and frustrated. They hadn't learned anything new from their trip to Colorado. Only that neither one of them smelled a familiar scent on the girl's clothes. All he wanted was a hot shower, food, and some rest before he went and saw Emily.

Walking into the house, he heard the noise and racket of numerous guests. So he probably wasn't going to get the nap.

He could still get the hot shower and food before going to see her. That was his plan when he started up the stairs, until he caught her scent in the air. She'd been in the house very recently. Even better. He would talk her into the shower with him.

He'd hated being away from her for three days. His mind kept returning to the run he'd shared with her. Chasing her as she ran, jumped, and teased. The feel of her fur and tongue when he'd finally caught her. They had laid in woods together, just taking in the sounds of nature. He'd watched her fall asleep and closed his eyes beside her.

He must have fallen asleep as well because the next thing he remembered it had been dark and they were both back in human form. She was spread over his body kissing his neck and chest.

His body hardened at the memory of her taking him deep inside. Riding him with the moonlight shining over her.

The words to ask to mate with her had been on the tip of his tongue when she'd dropped her head back and climaxed. The jolt that had gone through his body had sizzled him, and he had rolled her over to pound himself inside her until she came again, screaming, taking him with her.

Dropping his bag at the foot of the stairs, he headed to look for her. She needed to join him for a shower *now*.

Toby was in the kitchen, tying his shoes. "You're home!" he exclaimed.

Cain smiled. That was a good greeting, and he was expecting a better one from Emily.

"Hey, champ." He ruffled his hair. "How's it going?"

Toby smiled up at him, showing a missing tooth. "Good."

"Hey, there's something different about you." Cain stroked his chin, pretending to think about it. "Did you get your hair cut?"

Toby laughed and shook his head.

"Hmm, wonder what it is."

Toby smiled, his large gap in plain view.

They both turned as the kitchen door opened. Toby scowled and bent down to finish tying his shoes.

"Hey, just came in for some water. We got a football game in the back yard going," Kyle told them.

Toby mumbled something and jumped off the stool.

Cain nodded at Kyle and placed a hand on Toby's shoulder. They were silent until Kyle walked out the door.

"Okay, bud, let's figure this out." He studied Toby again. "It's not new shoes. Hmm, let's see..." Cain trailed off. Toby still had the scowl on his face. "What's up, bud?"

Toby looked down at the ground and kicked the cupboard. Cain waited patiently. When Toby finished thinking about what he wanted to say, he looked up at Cain with big eyes.

"I thought Emily was your girl," he told his older brother.

Cain nodded. "Does that bother you?"

Toby shook his head enthusiastically. "No, if she was your girl, she'd stay. Not go away again."

Cain nodded. "Okay."

Toby shifted from one foot to another. "But if she's your girl, how come Kyle was kissing her?"

Cain felt like he had been punched in the stomach. "Where?"

Toby tilted his head at him. "On the mouth."

Cain tried to hold his fury in. He looked at the young, innocent boy in front of him. "Where were they?"

"In the living room."

Cain nodded.

"I don't want her going away with him," Toby told him.

Cain gently ruffled his hair again. "She won't. Don't worry."

Cain gave him one last pat on the head and strode to the sliding glass door.

He saw her the minute he stepped out the door. His vision narrowed to only her. He crossed the yard quickly as she turned and smiled at him.

Emily sensed him more than knew he was there. She smiled, but as she turned, the smile almost immediately fell from her face. He looked furious. When he reached her, he grabbed her arm in an iron tight grip and yanked her towards the house.

"Hey!"

He dragged her forward so fast she tripped over her own feet. He held her up by her arm then half turned, picked her up, and threw her over his shoulder.

Emily was humiliated, but instead of causing a bigger scene, she let it go without fighting. He went through the open glass door, crossed the kitchen and kicked the swinging door open into the hall.

She cursed at him quietly, demanding he put her down. Emily couldn't believe he was acting this way as he stomped up the stairs and down the hall to his room. She started kicking and scratching when he opened the door then slammed it behind him. He dropped her on the bed none too gently.

"Cain?" Emily raised herself on her elbows.

"What the hell were you thinking, Emily?" he yelled.

She blinked. "Wh...what?"

He stood in front of the bed, and his eyes were flashing. She could feel the shimmering in the air as he tried not to shift.

"Why, Emily?"

"Cain, I don't know what you're talking about. Please just tell me what happened. What I did." She tried to keep her voice soft and controlled. She'd never seen him this way. She didn't know if it was something with what he was working on or her. But it scared her. He was pacing the room like... a caged wolf. "Cain, calm down."

"Don't! Do not tell me to calm down, Emily. Did you think I wouldn't find out? Did you think I would just shrug it off?" His voice had gone low, dangerously low.

"Find out what?" She moved more firmly up the bed. She didn't like where this was going. "Talk to me, Cain."

"Shut up. Just shut the hell up," he ordered still in that deadly tone. "What did you think I'd do, Emily?"

She didn't know what was going on, but for the first time in her life, she was afraid of him. She kept her mouth closed. Part from fear and the fact she couldn't believe he'd told her to shut up. That wasn't like him. Sure, he was domineering and arrogant, but he was never downright disrespectful.

"Answer me, damn it!"

"You told me to shut up," she blurted out. She hadn't meant to say it, but she was scared and starting to get pissed herself.

He was on her—from the door to the bed in one leap—and he sat with his knees holding her legs down and arms at her side.

"Cain." She struggled, which only seemed to make him madder.

He lifted her shoulders up and slammed them back on the bed hard. Her breath whooshed out of her.

"Cain, please!"

He did it again, and she felt the tears forming more from fear than pain.

"What? Wasn't expecting I wouldn't take it well?"

Emily shook her head. "Cain, please...you're hurting me."

He let go of her abruptly and backed away with a look that said he couldn't stand to touch her.

"Cain?"

He shook his head at her. "Go."

"What?"

He turned his cold eyes at her. "Go. Get out. I don't want to see you. Don't want to be around you."

She stood up slowly. "Cain."

"Get out!" he yelled at her.

She fumbled for the door while tears ran unchecked down her cheeks. She made it out the door and down the hall, but stopped as she ran into something solid.

"Emily." Kyle gripped her shoulders. "You okay?"

She nodded. She was numb. She had no idea what was going on. How could Cain turn on her? She'd been so looking forward to having him home.

"Did he hurt you?" Kyle asked her quietly.

She shook her head. Cain hadn't hurt her. He'd destroyed her. The look on his face was one she would never forget. She'd known he'd be home today and had hung around waiting for him. Then he flipped out and...

"Aww, isn't this sweet?" Cain's voice came up behind them.

Emily jumped and slammed her back into the wall. Kyle shifted slightly and had Cain raising an amused brow.

"Coming to her rescue?"

Kyle looked between Cain and Emily. "Just making sure she's okay."

Cain laughed. "Were you? Were you really?"

Cain's fist flew out and landed on Kyle's jaw. He didn't pull his punch and had Kyle going through the sheet rock on the wall. His head cracked against it, and the sheet rock fell in clumps around him.

Emily screamed and ran towards Kyle to help. Cain grabbed her arm before she reached him and pushed her back into the wall.

"Don't touch him," he ordered.

Emily looked up at him. "Cain. Please tell me what's wrong."

"Wrong?" His hand snaked up to her throat. "Why do you say something's wrong?"

Her eyes widened as she felt his hand tighten. "Cain," she managed.

"You're not laughing now, are you?" he asked. "Did you when he had his mouth on you? His hands?" he spat at her.

"No, Cain." She looked at him pleadingly. . "He didn't touch me, I swear!" The tears fell again. Why would he even think she would betray him? What had happened? "I didn't do anything."

He laughed. "Just couldn't wait to get another wolf between your legs." Cain moved in to cover her body with his. She was trapped between his body and the wall with his hand still around her throat.

"Let her go, Cain," Lamont said from behind Cain. He looked quickly over to Kyle and watched as he tried to sit up. Cain blocked Emily from his view, and Lamont knew he had to get them separated. Whatever had happened needed to be taken care of quickly, before someone got hurt badly.

Cain didn't turn, didn't acknowledge his Alpha.

"Cain," Lamont growled.

Finally, he turned his head but still held her.

"Cain, let go of Emily."

Cain just shook his head.

"That is an order from your Alpha," Lamont said loudly. He moved forward. "Now!"

Lamont watched Cain try to get control. His eyes were black, which Lamont had never seen before. As Cain blinked, they lightened.

He let go of Emily abruptly, and she sagged against the wall.

"Go to the study now," Lamont ordered.

Without looking at her, Cain headed down the stairs. Lamont knew Tony had followed him up and was standing behind him.

"Tony, help Kyle to the living room and take care of his injuries," Lamont said without turning around. He never took his eyes off Emily.

He walked slowly to her. She was shaking so badly her teeth were chattering.

"Come on, honey." He wrapped his arm around her and pulled her from the wall.

She dropped her chin but let him help her. "Kyle never touched me. I swear," she told him softly, her voice hoarse and the bruise around her neck red. She wasn't hurt though, just scared. Lamont's hands shook as he tried to remain gentle.

"I know, honey." He pulled her with him down the stairs.

He led her to the study. Cain had his back to them as they entered but knew they were there. Lamont gently ushered her to the couch. She sat and pulled her legs up to her chest and wrapped her arms around them.

Lamont went back to the door and closed and locked it. Cain stared out into the yard, and Emily had her chin on her knees.

He took his seat behind his desk. "Want to tell me what happened?"

Neither answered. He didn't think they would. He had a very good idea what was going on. His heart lifted a little thinking about it. And he knew his son. He knew how to get through to him.

"Okay, maybe you can tell me when you two mated, and why you didn't tell your Alpha or get his permission first."

Emily's head popped up, and Cain turned. Yes, that got their attention, he thought.

"We didn't, Lamont," Emily answered.

But Lamont wasn't looking at her, he was looking at Cain.

Cain nodded. "We did not. You should know better than that."

Lamont leant back in his chair. "And you should know better than to put your hands on a female."

Cain darted his eyes away. "I didn't mean to. I...I just couldn't stop."

Lamont looked over at Emily, who was rubbing her chin on her knees. "You remember Marc?" he asked.

They both nodded. Marc had been a young wolf only about five years older than Emily. He had found his mate with one of the young members of the Pack. Marc had come home to find his female with another Were and had killed them both.

"He'd gone into a rage when he'd found out his mate had betrayed him. To this day, he doesn't remember what he had done to them."

Emily sucked in a breath, and Cain's eyes narrowed. They could see where he was heading with his questions.

"We didn't mate," Cain told him.

Lamont believed that they hadn't intended to. They may not have exchanged blood. But he knew, could sense, that they were indeed mated.

"Yet you two are very much mated."

Cain laughed. "Mated. Soul mates," he said bitterly.

Lamont nodded. "It is also been said that when one mate betrays another, the pain from it can be blinding and result in things the injured mate would never normally do."

Cain shook his head. "She is not my mate."

Hurt flickered in Emily's eyes, but she quickly schooled her face.

"How'd she betray you, Cain?" Lamont asked him.

Cain turned his back again. He took a deep breath before looking back at his Alpha.

"She betrayed me with Kyle."

"I did not!" Emily yelled, jumping up from her seat.

Cain whirled on her. "Don't fucking lie to me. Toby saw you."

"Toby? Toby saw..." Her eyes widened and knowledge filled them.

Cain growled and took a step towards her.

"Cain," Lamont warned.

"Cain, it wasn't..." She put her hands up, but he turned his back on her.

Emily bit her lip and looked at Lamont. "I was playing Monopoly in the living room. Tony and Kyle came in, and I—"

Cain whipped around and had her by the arms. "So you admit it!"

"No!" She shook her head. "I mean, he came in and picked me up and...kissed me for like a second. Just hello. He's been doing it for years. That's all. I swear that's all."

"That's not all!"

"Yes, it is. I haven't been alone with Kyle. Not once."

She wasn't lying. Lamont could smell it and knew that Cain could too.

"I swear, Cain." She begged for him to believe her.

He shook his head. "I just... When Toby told me Kyle kissed you, I lost it."

"I'm so sorry," she said softly.

"Don't! Don't you fucking apologise to me!" Cain's eyes burned. He could have hurt her, killed her. Lamont heard his thoughts even if they weren't said out loud. "She needs to go back to school."

Emily's gasp was audible, but Lamont wasn't surprised.

"No," he told his son.

Cain looked him in the eye. "I am asking, as your son, send her back."

"Unprotected?"

Cain frowned, then rubbed his hand over his face. "No. Hell."

Emily's eyes had cleared and her voice was strong when she told them, "I don't have to be sent anywhere." She looked at Lamont. "I'm going home."

She walked out without permission from her Alpha. After she slammed the door, Cain looked at Lamont.

"I could have killed her."

Lamont nodded. "Yes. Now what are you going to do?"

"I don't know." His son confessed. "I wanted to mate with her. I almost asked her to but didn't."

Lamont stood and clasped his son's shoulder. "There have been a few instances when the exchange of blood hasn't been necessary. It's very rare, but it has happened."

"I didn't know." Cain laid his hand over his father's and squeezed. "I swear I didn't know."

Cain stepped away. Lamont gave him time to get his thoughts together. It took several minutes.

"It wasn't me... What I mean is, I knew what I was doing, but I felt disconnected somehow." Cain went on, "I couldn't stop myself. All I could see was red. I can't believe I hurt her."

"She'll be okay," Lamont assured him. "Most of her hurt is not physical."

"I don't deserve her," Cain's voice was full of hurt. "I never did."

Chapter Seven

Emily cried the entire way back to the cabin. So he didn't want her around. That was fine with her, she wouldn't be around then.

But it hurt. It hurt so much. Cain, the man she had always loved, had thought she would betray him. He didn't want her anymore. What they shared had been enough for him.

He wouldn't have to see her, she would make sure of that. She wiped her eyes with the back of her hands. And she wouldn't cry over him. She made it to the front door before she started crying again.

She opened the door and looked around the empty cabin. It was fully furnished with furniture, pictures, food, but it was lonely. She had always liked living alone, having her privacy, but right now it was just deadly quiet.

She walked to the bedroom, kicked off her shoes and climbed to the middle of the bed, curling up as she cried herself asleep.

Emily woke up drained. Her eyes were gritty, and her throat raw. Her stomach felt sick. Dragging herself out of bed, she went straight into the bathroom and climbed into the shower. She turned the water on as hot as she could stand it.

The shower and bathroom was done in a deep brown marble with large showerheads raining down. She placed both hands on the smooth wall of the shower and leant her forehead against it.

She didn't know how long she was in the shower, but when the water started to turn cold, she unhappily turned off the water. Dressed in pyjama pants and a tank top, she headed for the kitchen to make some tea to smooth her stomach.

She didn't turn on any lights, because she didn't need to, and the least amount of activity the better. She walked slowly and made it halfway into the kitchen, which opened to overlook the living room, before she saw him.

He sat in the chair next to the lamp that was on, watching her. Once he saw he had her attention, he stood.

She didn't ask how he got in. "What are you doing here?"

He didn't answer immediately.

"What do you want, Cain?" she asked. Her voice cracked, and she looked away.

He stepped towards her, but she stepped back, shaking her head. "Don't touch me. Just go away, Cain."

"I can't, Emily. You know I can't. I have to make this right."

She didn't look at him but shrugged. "Fine, it's fine. Now go away."

He stepped closer to her slowly. "Emily."

She shook her head and tried with all her might to hold back tears. "Go, Cain. I can't see you. Please."

He did touch her then. He moved and wrapped his arms around her, holding her close. She struggled, but he held on.

"Shh, please, please let me try to fix this," Cain begged.

"No… No… Just let go." Her voice broke, and he held her head on his shoulder and let her cry.

He picked her up and cradled her in his arms. "Oh baby, I'm sorry, so very sorry," he told her, rocking her.

"Y-y-you d-d-don't w-w-want me," she choked out.

"Baby, oh baby." He moved to sit on the couch, still holding her to him. "No, baby. Oh God, Emily."

"Y-y-you said…"

He laid his forehead on the top of her head. "Listen, just listen." He lifted her chin and looked into her eyes.

He leant in and kissed her tears away. "I'm in a new place here. I've never had these feelings before. I feel out of control…like I'm sinking."

Emily wiped her eyes and took a deep breath. She was embarrassed that she couldn't stop crying. She tried to pull away, but he held her.

"Don't, baby. Please let me hold you."

Emily watched him a moment. "Why?"

Cain frowned. "Why? I want to feel you. I want to touch you."

"You wanted to send me away," she accused.

"I did," he admitted, and her eyes teared up again. "I've had feelings for you for so long that I couldn't act on. I finally have you, and then I hurt you. I could have killed you, Emily. Do you understand that?"

She sighed. "Do you think what Lamont said is true?"

Cain shook his head. "I don't know." He tightened his grip around her when she shifted. "Does it matter?"

She nodded. "I don't want to be with someone who doesn't really want me. If you're here just because your dad made you come, then you need to leave. If you don't want me then...then that's fine, but you have to leave me alone then."

He kissed her lightly on the lips, rubbing softly. "Emily, my dad did not tell me to come here. He doesn't even know I am. He's probably figured it out, but I don't care. This is about you and me. I hurt you, baby, and I have to make up for that."

She pushed away and he let her finally. She stood in front of him. "You feel guilty."

"Yes. I had no right to put my hands on you out of anger."

Emily gave him a sad smile. "Go, Cain."

He reached out and grabbed her hands. "Emily."

But Emily pulled them away. "No. I don't want you because you feel guilty. I've been in love with you for eight years. Maybe it was fated, or maybe it wasn't. I don't care about you grabbing me. I just want you to love me. I want you to choose me, Cain."

He stood and put a hand under her chin. She met his eyes, as he wanted. "Do you remember what I said to you that first day? Before I made love with you."

She nodded.

"Say it."

"Mine. You said I was yours."

He stepped closer. "That was just me talking to you. I meant it then, and I still do. You are mine, Emily. I choose you and still want you." He kissed her gently, just a soft meeting of lips before picking her up.

"Let me prove it to you." He took her into the bedroom and laid her gently on the bed.

He made love to her slowly and gently, putting all the feelings he had for her in the open. Emily knew it was the only way he had to show her.

His lips lingered over her body, his tongue worshipped her skin, and his fingers traced across her so lightly it was barely a touch. Cain whispered sweet nothings in her ear as he seduced her body and mind.

The love she felt for him was reflected with every caress. Tears welled up, and for the first time in her life, she felt truly adored and protected.

When he slipped inside, she wrapped around him, taking all of him in. He kept his strokes slow and deep, and when her eyes went unfocused and she breathed out his name, he linked their fingers, leant in, and kissed her as they came together.

* * * *

Lamont hung up the phone with a feeling of dread.

There had been another attack. This time in Montana, this time had been more brutal, and this time it had been on Pack territory. Shaking his head, he looked out the window into the darkness.

A meeting had been called for all the Packs. It would take place in Colorado in Riker's territory. He had to send Cain, and while his son could handle it, how would it affect his relationship with Emily?

Lamont had suspected for a while now that they might be fated to mate. No two had ever fought it as hard as they did, but you couldn't miss the emotions when the two were together.

He hadn't believed Cain would hurt Emily until he saw them that day.

Cain had more control of his emotions than any wolf he'd known, including himself. It had been when Lamont had heard her scream at the stairs that he'd known something was wrong.

He hadn't punished Cain. Cain would be doing that to himself. Sometimes being a father was harder than being an Alpha. He had to protect them both, even if that meant protecting Cain from himself. Lamont was sure that Cain would punish himself ten times worse than Lamont would have.

He glanced at his watch. It was ten-thirty, and he didn't expect Cain back tonight. If they worked things out, Cain would be an idiot to leave her tonight. If they did not, Cain still wouldn't return. He would be off torturing himself. Lamont wanted to reach out to his son. He wanted to offer his reassurances, but he knew Cain wouldn't accept them. Cain had to work out his own feelings.

He looked up as the knock came on the study door.

Tony walked in and nodded politely. "You got a minute?"

Nodding, Lamont gestured to the chair in front of him.

Tony rubbed his hands on his pants and took a deep breath. "What are you going to do about Cain?"

Lifting his eyebrow at his middle son, Lamont did not answer.

"I mean. If you see fit to punish him, well, I'd understand, but..."

"Just say it, Tony."

"I should probably be punished too," Tony finished quietly.

Lamont sat back in his chair. This he hadn't been expecting. "Want to tell me why?"

Tony sighed heavily. "I knew about the first time they...were together. I was eating in the kitchen when they came up from the gym. I also knew how Cain would react to her friendship with Kyle. I didn't warn Kyle. I thought... I just wanted to give him a nudge. You know, to make a move. I don't know two more perfect..."

"Mates?" Lamont finished and Tony nodded.

"So should I punish Toby?"

Tony's eyes widened. "No, that's not what I meant."

"Well, if I punish you for knowing Cain would be jealous of Kyle, then shouldn't I punish Toby for telling Cain about it?"

Tony would know where his father was going with this. "No."

Lamont nodded at him. "Honourable for you to feel guilty, but unnecessary. Cain is responsible for his own actions."

Tony nodded again. "He wouldn't have hurt her. Not like that. He doesn't have it in him. He loves her. I can feel it when he's with her."

"Yes."

"I just don't understand what happened."

Lamont reached over and tried to give his son the only help he could. "I believe that Cain and Emily mated."

Tony jumped up to come to his brother's rescue. His mouth opened and closed as he sputtered out an argument. It was a crime to mate or bond without the Alpha's permission. Lamont gestured him back down.

"I don't believe they knew."

It took a moment, but the realisation at what Lamont was saying came through.

"You think they were fated?"

Lamont only nodded.

Tony digested that information for a minute. "It would make sense."

They sat there for a moment.

"So what else is bothering you?" Tony asked him.

Lamont smiled. Tony could read people even without his enhanced features.

"There was another attack. A special meeting has been called. I have to send Cain."

Tony nodded. "And he just got back today, and this happened."

Lamont nodded. "I'll give him tonight with her. He'll have to be back in Colorado the day after tomorrow."

Chapter Eight

Emily was wrapped around him, her head cushioned on his shoulder and her arm around him with her hand resting on his chest, one long slim leg thrown between his.

Cain realised then that he had never actually slept all night with a female before.

He stroked a hand down her arm to her waist. He had an overwhelming feeling to take Emily to his bed. To prove to himself that she was different. She would not leave him.

His cell phone rang, and she shifted, rubbing her face against his chest with a moan. It was six in the morning, and she really wasn't a morning person. Cain knew who it would be before he reached to the floor where his pants had fallen.

Taking his cell phone out of his pocket, he opened it and answered his father's call.

"Hello?"

He started rubbing his fingers through Emily's hair absently as he listened to his dad talk. She moved her head slightly and placed a row of small kisses on his chest. His hand tightened in her hair, and she laughed softly.

He finished talking to his dad then turned to her as he closed his phone.

"There was another attack?" she asked him.

He reached over for her hand and lifted it to his lips. "Yes, in Montana." He watched her eyes widen. "A meeting has been set up for all of us in Colorado. I have to go, Emily."

"I know."

"Emily." He held her hand tight. "I want..." He shook his head. He couldn't give her orders. "Would you please stay in the main house? In my room."

She looked down at the sheets that were tangled around her legs. "Because of the attacks?"

"Partly. The attack happened on Pack territory this time. She was in one of the houses, and he got her there. I don't want you here alone. That's why I want you in the main house. I want you in my bedroom because it's *my* bedroom. I've never had a woman stay in my room, ever. I want you in it. I want you to be different. And not just while I'm gone." He rubbed his thumb on her wrist. He felt her pulse quicken.

She smiled at him. "Good answer."

He leaned over and kissed her. "And your answer?"

She pretended to think about it until he laughed and pulled her on top of him. He kissed her, his hands caressing down her back to her bottom.

"Mmm, when do you leave?" she asked, straddling his waist.

He pushed up, moving his hand in circles until he cupped her breast, then bent to take her nipple in his mouth. She moaned, and he flipped her on her back.

"Oh, we have a little bit of time."

An hour later, they were arguing in her living room.

"But I don't need all my stuff now. I can come back and get what I need."

He shook his head. "You're not returning alone."

She sighed. "Okay, I'll bring Tony with me."

It was logical, but he wanted to see her stuff mixed in with his before he left. He wanted that reminder that she would be there when he returned. "It will make me feel better if I knew you had everything you need."

She looked at him suspiciously. "Cain, you're not thinking about doing something stupid like locking me inside the main house, are you?"

He'd thought about it. He knew it would never work, but honestly, he had thought about it. "No, not locking you in the house. The main yard is fine, and if you want to go for a run, take Tony with you. Just don't leave the main house alone."

"Cain. When you come back?"

He was throwing her books in a bag and looked up. "What?"

She shrugged. "I was just wondering how long I was going to stay in your room."

He frowned, not understanding what she was asking. Hadn't they already discussed this? "It's your room now, too."

"But what about when I go back to school?"

He straightened slowly from where he was trying to get her stuff together. "You're not going back."

He watched her back go up and her eyes narrow. He hadn't really thought about it. He'd just guessed now that they were together she wouldn't want to go back.

"Cain."

He slung the bag over his shoulder and picked up the two bags of clothes and bathroom products. "Let's go."

She didn't move. "Cain, I only have one semester to go. I need to finish school."

He shook his head. "I'm sorry, Emily. I really am, but it's just not possible." With that, he walked out of the room.

It only took her a minute to follow and be on his heels. "We need to talk about this." She followed him through the house and out the door.

He didn't speak until he threw her bags in the back of the truck. "If there was any way to have you finish, baby, I would. But it's just not logical. I can't leave here. This is my place. I have to be here to take care of Pack business and protect Lamont. I can't do that hours away."

"Yes, but I could go—"

He interrupted her. "Baby, stop and think about what you were going to say. What? You'll go and finish? I wouldn't be able to let you out of my sight for that long. And you would be a walking target as an Enforcer's mate alone. No, that's not going to happen. And you need to think about our future. Together."

"Our future?"

He cupped her chin, lifting her face up. "Emily, I am going to want to do the mating ritual soon, and after that the bonding ceremony. I want you officially mine."

"Cain, I am yours. But if we just waited…"

"No, Emily. I know it's not fair, but this is what you're getting. I'm an Enforcer. I am second-in-command of our Pack. This is me. And it will have to be you too." He leant down and kissed her gently. "Now, you have enough to think about, and I have to go pack my bag. Come on, let's go."

Cain could feel Emily fighting her emotions as he got in the truck to take her home. It would be her home, and he knew she would have to adjust to it. To the people and the noise. But it's what she had wanted. It was the only way they would be able to be together.

He wanted her to finish school and knew it was important to her. But he couldn't see how she would be able to.

Toby was playing outside in the front lawn when they pulled up. He started to run to the truck and stopped as if he'd remembered the scene yesterday.

God, had it only been yesterday? Everything was changing so fast.

Seeing Toby, Cain turned to Emily. "Emily, he didn't mean… What I mean is, if you could take it easy on Toby…"

She sent him a sidewise look and rolled her eyes. "I'm not heartless, Cain. I know Toby didn't mean any harm."

Cain took her hand. "He was scared you were going to leave again. This time with Kyle."

She looked back at the young boy who was kicking rocks, his hands in his pockets, and her heartstrings tugged. "Let me talk to him."

Cain grinned at her and jerked her forward for a kiss. "I'll put your things in my…our room."

Emily approached Toby slowly. Looking over her shoulder, judging the hearing distance from Cain, she asked softly, "Got a minute?"

Toby nodded but didn't look at her. She sat cross-legged on the grass and took off her flip-flops. "I love this time of year. When the grass is so thick you can run your feet through it," Emily told him.

"Are you leaving? Is that why Cain has your bags?" Toby blurted out.

She held a hand out to him. "Come here please, Toby."

He came to her reluctantly. She pulled him to sit on her lap and adjusted him so she could see his face. " I guess you're pretty upset about what happened yesterday, huh?"

Toby just shrugged.

Emily continued. "Yeah, me and your brother had a pretty big fight. I bet that scared you."

Another shrug.

Emily sighed. "Toby, Cain and I have a complicated relationship. I don't really understand it myself."

What was there to understand? Cain asked himself as he eavesdropped on Emily and Toby from the porch. She was his. There, easy! Tony opened the door and started to ask him what he was doing, but Cain hushed him quickly. Tony rolled his eyes and was going to shut the door when Emily spoke again.

"Sometimes when we don't know how to say what we want, we yell."

Cain couldn't see them, but he could picture Emily with Toby on her lap.

"But Cain did more than yell."

Cain sighed and turned to head towards the two of them when Tony caught his arm. Tony shook his head at him.

"Let her take care of this," he said quietly.

Emily did. "And you think that's your fault."

"Did you get hurt because of me?"

Cain knew she would be hugging him now.

"I'm not hurt. Cain didn't really hurt me. He scared me. That's all. But I understand why and you need to too."

Toby nodded. "Because I told him Kyle kissed you."

Emily surprised them all with her next statement. "Toby, you did the right thing."

"I did?" Toby asked, and Cain and Tony exchanged confused looks.

"Who do you trust more than anyone you know to help you and protect you?" she asked him.

"Lamont."

"And then?"

"Cain and Tony."

"Good. You see? You had a worry. You thought maybe I would leave. So you told one of the people you trust the most so they could fix it, right?"

"I thought Cain could make you stay."

"I am staying. But Toby, Cain didn't make me stay. I chose to stay."

Toby laughed happily. "I don't care why as long as you do. I've got to tell Lamont and Tony."

Emily stood laughing. "Tony already knows. He's listening from the porch with Cain, but you can tell Lamont."

Tony and Cain exchanged an amused look and stepped inside.

Cain felt his whole body tingle with the awareness that Emily had said she would stay. She had committed herself.

Chapter Nine

The drive was long to Colorado, but Cain knew he had something to look forward to getting home to. Emily had been awake to see him leave and kissed him goodbye. The sight of her in her robe standing at the door was one Cain would cherish during his time away.

Adam had been silent for most of the trip. They had stopped for coffee fifteen miles back, and Cain took over the driving.

"How's your dad doing?" Cain asked his friend.

Cain and Adam had been best friends growing up. When Lamont offered Christian his own Pack and territory, it was the first time the two friends had ever been apart.

Adam sighed heavily before answering. "Still depressed and blaming himself. It seems the only one who can reach him is Logan."

"Logan's been staying at your house?" Cain asked.

"Yeah." Adam sighed. "Logan and Dad have been friends for a long time, since before I was even born.

Dad doesn't have a mate, so I'm glad he at least has his friend. I'm not sure what's going to happen."

"Not his fault," Cain commented.

"I know, but he blames himself. He thinks she should have been in territory, and it wouldn't have happened."

"The last attack happened in territory."

"Try telling him that." Adam's laugh was bitter. "I'm thankful for the help, though. Logan is a good guard. With me being gone so much, I feel better having him around."

Cain rubbed his hand over his face. "Can't be easy being an Alpha. I know Lamont is always the last one to bed and the first one up."

Adam stared out the window. "He wants me to take over the Pack."

Cain wasn't surprised. Most Alphas left their Packs to their sons. "You'd be a good Alpha."

Adam finally looked at him. "Do you think so?"

Cain didn't hesitate with his answer. "Yes, I do. You would be a fair leader. A good leader. One of the reasons Lamont gave Christian a Pack was knowing that someday you would take it."

Adam gave him a small smile. "I'm worried when Logan leaves that Dad might want to end his existence."

Cain knew Weres who had done that. Not many did but some. Usually after they lost their mate. Both his mother and Kyle's had died in a car accident when they were children, but luckily their dads had stayed around to raise them.

"Maybe he won't," Cain offered, not knowing what else to say.

"I guess we'll find out soon. Logan got word that his Alpha is expecting his first child. He'll need to return to guard over them."

Cain smiled. He had always liked Logan's Alpha, Gage. Gage's mate was one of the few Weres who couldn't shift. He understood she'd had a hard childhood, but when he met her for the first time, the love she had for her mate was obvious.

Thinking of Gage having a child made him think of Emily. She would be a great mother. The way she was with Toby was proof of that.

It was something they needed to discuss. He could picture their children running around playing while he held her in his arms.

* * * *

Cain knew the minute he walked into the meeting that it wasn't like the others he had attended. The different Pack's representatives were all edgy and looking at each other with suspicion.

Cain took in the others in the room as he sat in one of the offered chairs.

Riker sat at the head of a long conference table. He was the only actual Alpha in attendance, so he would be in charge of the meeting.

Cain had taken the seat next to Sam, who was a guard and third-in-command with Gage. With the new Alpha expecting their first child, Cain knew Gage's Pack was stretched thin. Extra precautions would be taken with Gage's mate, and that would require extra guards.

If he didn't have Emily at home waiting for him, Cain might have offered to accompany Sam back to his territory.

Cain watched as the room filled up quickly. There were nine territories being represented today. Riker started the meeting as soon as everyone had taken a seat. It was agreed upon that the attacks most likely had been done by another Were.

The survivors had all gave the same description. The attacker had only wanted one thing from them. After he attacked the girls, he would beat them with his fists. The beatings had rapidly gotten worse until the last victim hadn't lived through it.

In the middle of the meeting, Riker's second entered and stood behind his Alpha. Cain didn't know much about Larry. Unlike most Packs, Riker made the males of his Pack fight for position. An Alpha could tell dominance inside a wolf without the need for violence. However, a few Alphas still let Pack rank be held by earning it.

Cain watched Larry as he watched the room until finally their eyes met.

Cain took an immediate dislike to the man. There was no compassion in the second's eyes as Adam spoke about the results of Mindy's attack.

Sam shifted beside him, and Cain noticed he was also staring at Larry. Sam tilted his head, and Cain got the impression he was scenting him.

Larry's eyes narrowed at Sam as he sneered back.

Sam sat back in his chair as if nothing was up, but Cain made a mental note to get together with him once the meeting was over.

Sam was leaning against the car when Cain walked up with Adam. He straightened and nodded towards them as they approached.

Cain shook hands with him then moved aside for Adam. Other Packs were leaving as Cain acknowledged Brent Simpson. They waved at one another in greeting. He'd only met the man once when Cain had made his first and only trip to California. Brent had been the one to show him around, and although Cain wouldn't say they were friends, Brent was a nice enough guy.

As the parking lot started to thin out, Cain turned to Sam and Adam. "This meeting didn't do anything. Everyone is still blaming each other, and we didn't find out anything new."

"Gage calls it political bullshit, but it had to be done. Otherwise, the Packs will start to rip each other apart," Sam said.

"Damn." Cain ran his hand over his face. He was tired and just wanted to be with Emily. "We need to end this fast. Did you get anything from scenting Larry?"

Sam smiled, but shook his head. "No. His scent wasn't one I recognised, but I could have sworn it was in the room."

Cain hadn't wanted to say anything, but he agreed. "So you think it is someone who was at the meeting?"

"Son of a bitch." Adam growled. "And we let him go?"

Cain put his hand on Adam's shoulder to calm him. "We don't know that it was. But it gives us an idea. We do know who was at the meeting, and that gives us a place to start."

Adam shrugged off his hand. "That's going to do a lot of good for the next girl."

Sam moved restlessly, and Cain knew he could tell how close Adam was to shifting. "It gives us something," he told his old friend.

Adam took several deep breaths before nodding. "Sorry."

Sam slapped him on the back. "Had me worried there for a second. Well, I've got to run. Marissa is driving Gage crazy with all her cravings, so in turn, he's driving me crazy sending me after things. I have instructions to stop on my way home and pick up a list a mile long. I tell you, I don't think I want children after seeing this."

All three men laughed and waved goodbye. Getting in the car, Cain looked over at Adam.

"You okay?"

"Yeah, but if we think it's Larry, why don't we just go after him?"

Sounded like a plan to him, but Cain knew they couldn't, not just yet. "Because if it's not, it would start a Pack war, and we don't need that on top of this."

"Just so you know, I'm going to rip this guy apart when we find him," Adam said quietly.

"Okay." With that said, he started the long drive home.

Chapter Ten

Emily ran around the large tree and pulled her shirt over her head. She had long ago learned not to be shy about her naked body, but she didn't think that Cain would much like his brother seeing her that way.

She'd been restless all day waiting for Cain to return. She didn't like being away from him. It also made her realise that she couldn't go back to school with him staying inside the territory.

She needed a good long run to calm herself. The wolf inside was scratching to get out. Finally, she had been able to talk Tony into taking her out. She didn't like having to have a chaperon, but she did understand it. If Cain came back, and she'd been hurt, there would be no telling what he would do. Or how many people would end up hurt.

Why that thought made her happy she wasn't quite sure, but she decided to go with it.

After folding her clothes and placing them against the trunk of the tree, she knelt and welcomed the magic that would allow her to shift.

The tingling started at the tip of her toes and moved over her body quickly. Her skin grew tight, until it felt like it would burst. Bones adjusted inside her, and she felt herself float like she always did.

Then, only minutes later, she stood on all fours, tilted her head back, and yowled in pleasure. An answering call from the west told her that Tony was ready. She bounded for him, content to run and play until her man came home to her.

After dropping Adam off, Cain drove faster than the posted speed limit signs. He couldn't shake the feeling that something wasn't right. Picking up his cell phone from the middle console, he tried once again to reach Emily.

It rang four times before he got the message she couldn't answer at this time but to leave his name and number. Dread filled his stomach as he tried his brother. No answer there either.

Cain stomped his foot harder on the accelerator, and the car shot forward. They should be answering. He had told her to stay in the main house except if Tony was with her.

Of course, if she was in trouble, and Tony was with her, that might explain why neither was answering. Cain took the next turn too sharply, and the car skidded. Correcting the vehicle, he took a deep breath and slowed down. Getting himself killed wasn't going to help either of them.

His cell phone rang from where he thrown it in the seat beside him, causing him to swerve again in surprise. The number of the house showed on the I.D.

"Emily!" he answered.

"No, it's your father. What's wrong, Cain? I can feel your unease from here." His father's voice was soft but sharp, pulling him out of his panic.

Cain laughed almost hysterically. Why hadn't he thought of calling the house? Of course his father could sense when he was worried, so why wouldn't he be able to sense if Tony was in trouble?

"Cain, are you okay?" his father asked again.

"Yes. Yes, I'm fine. I couldn't get a hold of Emily or Tony, and I started to freak out. I didn't even think of calling you," he tried to explain.

His father's sigh of relief was audible even over the phone. "Emily and Tony are both fine. She was so restless waiting on your return that they went for a run."

That made Cain feel better, but he just wanted to be absolutely sure she was okay. "Can you sense them?"

When his father remained silent, Cain knew he was trying.

"Yes. Emily is very happy right now, and I believe she is outrunning your brother."

Cain could picture Emily in her small timber wolf body running from the bigger black wolf. While his brother was big and powerful, Emily was smaller and faster. She had almost outrun Cain the first time they'd gone out.

"Thanks. I'm only about thirty minutes away, but I could feel something wasn't right." He still had that feeling, but it had lessened. He still felt on edge, just that something wasn't right.

"It's probably just your bond. You've been away from her for too long. I'll have Kyle go tell them you're almost here."

Cain felt a growl try to escape from the back of his throat at the mention of the other man.

"Cain." His name came out as a warning.

He shook his head to clear his mind. "That would be great." Then he hung up and once again sped home to his waiting mate.

Cain pulled to the gates and waved to the guard inside. Antonio waved back as he pressed the button to let him in. Cain looked in his rear view mirror, still uneasy.

The drive to the house seemed to take hours even though it was less than ten minutes. He had his seat belt off before the car came to a complete stop.

Lifting his head to the wind, he concentrated on the sounds and smells around him. Then, using the mating bond, he tried to find Emily.

He could sense her behind the house still in wolf form. She was only about a mile away. He started to go to the house until another smell reached him. One mixed with hers. He knew that smell. It had been at the meeting.

Cain took off running while pulling at his clothes. He shifted as he ran which was as painful as it could get. Once on his four feet, he could run faster. That didn't stop the black and grey wolf from coming up from behind and passing him. So Lamont could sense the trouble too.

He picked up speed and ran next to his father into the woods. His ears picked up a loud growl then a whimper. He ran faster, jumping over fallen branches instinctively as he headed in the direction of Emily.

When he and his father broke through to where the sound of battle was already taking place, he immediately sought Emily.

His brother, in wolf form, was fighting a larger wolf while another went from snapping at the strange wolf to blocking Emily from it.

Lamont howled and headed into the fight. The strange wolf threw his brother off his back and met his father.

Cain ran to Emily to make sure she was okay. Her small frame was hunched down and little whimpers were escaping her. The wolf guarding her moved aside as Cain approached. Looking in his eyes and smelling him, Cain knew who he was. But if Larry was the wolf protecting Emily, who was his father now fighting?

Cain nuzzled Emily's neck and could have cried himself when her small tongue licked his paw. He shifted away from her and nodded at Larry.

The other wolf understood and moved to stand guard in front of her once again. Cain next checked on his brother who was lying on his side, panting. Tony was injured but alive. He turned to the wolf that now stood muzzle to muzzle with his Alpha.

Lamont darted in and nipped at him, but the other wolf was faster. Cain waited patiently while Lamont distracted him until the perfect moment. Then he jumped, knocking the other wolf off its feet, causing him to roll. He tried to regain all fours again, but Cain pounced and held him down.

They rolled, teeth clashing, as they both tried to get the upper hand. Distantly, Cain could hear Emily's whines and his father taking care of Tony, but he couldn't look back and give up his attention on the attacker.

The wolf made a move to get his back legs under Cain. It was just what he had been waiting for. Adjusting his body weight, Cain got a hold of the wolf's neck. He slammed him down hard once, then again. His sharp canines sunk farther into the fur until the other wolf gave up.

Going limp, he submitted to Cain.

Cain remained on alert as other members of his Pack—both in wolf and human forms—joined them. It was Antonio who spoke quietly to Cain, telling him to release. But the wolf inside Cain wouldn't let him. Instinct told him to rip the wolf's throat out for endangering its mate.

Then his father was there in human form, adding his voice to Antonio's. But it wasn't until Emily dropped next to him, human and naked, and placed her hand on his head that he could.

Letting go of the wolf, Cain crawled into her lap and started his own shift back, staring into her eyes the entire time.

Chapter Eleven

Cain held Emily in his arms as she shivered. Antonio had taken off his shirt and jacket and given them to her until he could return with her clothes, which Cain was grateful for. He was raw enough without having to think about her naked in front of everyone.

He still could not believe that the attacker had been Brent Simpson. He turned and glared at the other non-Pack member present.

"You knew," he accused Larry.

"I had my suspicions," the other man told him, shrugging. "I wasn't sure, so I decided to follow him when we left the meeting."

Cain was still shaking with rage at the thought of any man putting his hands on his mate. Emily's soft hand turned his head towards her.

"He saved me, Cain. I had gotten separated from Tony when he went to investigate another smell. I was trying to make my way back to my clothes when the other wolf appeared in front of me."

Cain tightened his hold on her.

"He came out of nowhere. One minute he was standing in front of me, and the next, he attacked."

"Shh…" Cain ran one hand over the back of her hair, letting the silk fall through his fingers.

"No, I want to tell you," she insisted.

Cain nodded, knowing she needed to get out what happened.

"He had me pinned down, and I really thought he was going to kill me. Then, all of a sudden, he was gone. Larry had pulled him off of me, and they started fighting. Then Tony ran in and joined the fight." Tears welled up in her eyes. "I'm so sorry, Cain. I just wanted to run."

"Oh, baby, it's not your fault." Cain let her bury her head in his chest as she cried. He looked up and met Larry's gaze.

"Thank you." It wasn't enough. It would never be enough to him. But this man, who he had suspected, had saved his mate's life.

Larry shrugged and half-smiled. "I should have told you what I thought, but I didn't know for sure. Besides, I don't think anyone would have believed me."

"Why not tell your Alpha?" Lamont asked, walking up and handing Cain Emily's clothes, which Antonio had found not far away.

Larry barked out a laugh. "Things run a little different in my Pack. If Riker had come into what you had, he would have watched the fight and then offered the winner a job."

"Sounds like you need a new Alpha," Cain commented.

The shadow that crossed Larry's face was brief, but he had seen it.

"Maybe I do," he whispered softly. He looked around the area surrounded with family and friends, his face showing a bit of longing. Then he backed away until he blended in with the trees and was gone.

* * * *

"Cain?" Emily rolled over and reached for him as she called out his name. The bed beside her was empty. She sat up and saw him sitting on the end of the bed.

"Cain?" She moved up behind him and wrapped her arms around his neck, pressing her breasts into his back. "What's wrong?"

"What's wrong?" He laughed out bitterly. "You could have been killed yesterday while I wasn't even here."

Emily sighed and crawled onto his lap. "I could have been killed even if you had been here."

He shook his head. "He knew I was with Adam, and he could beat me here. He went after you because you're my mate."

Emily understood. "And you blame yourself."

"Of course I do." Guilt laced his words.

She placed her hands on either side of his face and made him look at her. "You love me." When he started to respond, she put her fingers over his lips. "You love me, and you're afraid because of that I'll get hurt."

When he didn't deny it, Emily knew she was right. "But here's another thing. I love you too. I love you so much that when you're gone, I find myself going crazy thinking about you." She placed a soft kiss against his lips as she moved her hand. "There's always going to be danger, Cain. Whether I'm with you or not. I'd rather know that you'll always be looking out for me than have you push me away because of it."

"That's just it though. I'm so selfish that I would rather have you in danger than give you up."

Emily smiled, hoping he would understand. "I need to be with you, Cain. Always. I don't want you to ever give me up."

He visibly relaxed and under her bottom started to come to life. She wiggled and nipped his bottom lip. "Seems to me someone is feeling better."

With strong hands, he cupped her ass and pulled her tighter against him, her wet sex sliding over his skin. "I'll show you just what I'm feeling." And he kissed her.

Emily had never known a kiss to be so sweet and promising in her whole life. He drugged her with his caresses and tenderness.

Cain broke away, and she tried to follow. "One more thing."

"Enough talk," she demanded, reaching to fist his hard cock.

"Just have to tell you this..." he panted as she started to stroke him.

"What?"

"I talked to my father last night. We're going to promote Antonio to Enforcer so he can take the out-of-town jobs."

Emily's hand stilled. "You're staying here with me permanently." Joy filled her at the thought of not having to be separated from him again.

"Well, no."

Emily's heart jumped in her chest. "No? But you just said you wouldn't give me up."

He looked at her for a full minute before a smile broke out of his face. "I'm not."

"But…I don't understand."

"I'm going back to school with you. You'll finish the semester and then we'll return here together. To our home."

"Cain!" Emily smothered him with kisses.

He grabbed her face and their eyes locked. "I would do anything for you, honey. And this is just a small thing. You want to finish school, so I want to support you."

Once again, tears fell down her face.

"No crying! This is a good thing," he complained.

Emily scrubbed the tears from her face with the back of her hand. "Happy tears, Cain. You've made me so happy!"

"I'll always try to make you happy. But, when we return, I will take my post back as Enforcer for the territory. Are you okay with that?"

"Yes! Yes! I know that's who you are. I understand that!"

"Okay, then enough talk."

She squealed as he flipped their positions, so she was on her hands and knees on the bed and his hard body was over her.

"I also want to start a family after you're finished with school."

"A family?" Emily's breath caught as he teased the entrance of her pussy with his thick erection.

"Yes, a family. So we need to practice making one." With those words, he thrust deep inside her.

Her head fell forward as he started to pound into her from behind. Sensations ran rampant through her body as each stroke took her higher. A family. She would finally have a family.

"But we also need to take care of one more thing," he told her, not slowing the force of his strokes.

Emily couldn't believe he could talk right then. "Hmm?"

"I asked my father permission to mate officially."

Emily's body tightened and she knew she was close. "Mmm."

"Say yes. Say you want to mate with me," he ordered.

Emily slammed back into him. "Yessss..." she hissed her agreement. She felt his canines against her neck. "Yes."

He pierced her skin as she screamed out his name and her body exploded.

PACK TERRITORY

Dedication

This book is dedicated to the members of my yahoo
group.
Thanks for all the kind words and encouragement.

Chapter One

Adam White stretched his arms out as he walked up the back steps to his house. The late night run in his other form had done a remarkable job of relaxing him.

Opening the sliding glass door to enter the house, Adam took a deep breath and sensed the interior. His sister Laura was in the kitchen baking for the family and other guests who were sure to stop in. He smiled at the smell of cakes and cookies. His sister always cooked enough food for an army, and his mouth watered in anticipation.

He calmly took another breath and found the man he was searching for. His father and former Pack Alpha was in his room. Adam wasn't surprised. Christian spent all of his time either in his room or in his other form. Adam had tried to talk to him, to bring him out of the depression, but nothing he said or did helped.

Three months before, one of the young females of the Pack had been attacked. Mindy hadn't been the first or the only girl, but she was the only one from *their* Pack. Christian had to live with the knowledge that he hadn't been able to protect a Pack member.

Adam, Laura, and many Pack members—even other Alphas—had told Christian it wasn't his fault, but he continued to blame himself. The only person who seemed to be able reach him at all was his friend, Logan.

Logan had been staying at the house and talking with Christian daily, slowly bringing him back. But when Logan's Alpha, Gage, had found out that his mate was pregnant, Logan had to leave and return to his own territory. As expected, Gage's Pack was in high alert to make certain nothing happened to the Alpha's mate or child. Adam could understand the need, but he selfishly wished Logan could have stayed longer.

Adam headed to his office. For now, at least, his father was alive. Adam just needed to make sure he remained that way. It wasn't unusual for shifters to want to end their existence after a tragedy. Living for so long and witnessing so much affected each of them.

Opening the door to the Alpha's office, Adam stepped inside and flipped on the light. He had taken his new position only two months before and hadn't changed anything in the office or the house. He didn't know if he ever would.

The council, made up of former Alphas who policed the Packs, had given their blessing for him to take over the Pack, but Adam still had doubts whether he was ready. It was a huge responsibility and he didn't want to disappoint anyone, especially his father. The fact that he still needed to appoint his second-in-command weighed heavy on his mind.

He'd thought long and hard about who would be good for the position. Every Alpha picked his own man to watch his back. His father's man had stayed when Adam took over, but Adam knew he was more than ready to retire.

As he reached the desk, he turned on the computer and waited for it to boot up. As he sat, there was a knock on the door. He tried not to be annoyed at the interruption, but it was hard. He'd been hoping to have a little time to himself at the late hour. He wanted to finish going through the applications for his Enforcer. He had put it off long enough.

Tasha Johnson followed the guard inside the Alpha's house and down the hall. When they reached a large oak door, she ran her sweaty palms over her jeans. She hated to bring her family problems to the new Alpha, but she didn't know where else to turn.

The low voice that told them to enter sent a shiver down her spine. She braced herself for the meeting.

The guard opened the door and nodded at her to stay. Procedure dictated that she wait while she was announced and the Alpha decided whether or not to grant her an audience. Tasha wasn't too worried. Like his father before him, Adam was already known for making time for members of his Pack. As the guard walked away, she peeked inside and got a good look at the new Pack leader.

She'd known Adam for years, even though they'd never been close, and had admired him from a distance for a long time now. The fact that she was about face him alone made her stomach flutter with nerves.

Adam nodded as the guard spoke quietly to him before looking up and locking gazes with her. His light green eyes held hers and her breath rushed out of her chest at the intensity with which he watched her.

Then he smiled and liquid arousal pooled inside her panties. She shifted to relieve the pressure, certain if she didn't calm her body, he would be able to tell. Oh, the man just oozed raw sexuality.

When he stood and motioned her in, she didn't miss the large bulge trapped in his jeans. The sight of his excitement did nothing to tame her own desire. She wasn't sure if he was reacting to her or not, but a woman could hope. Secretly, she wished he wanted her as much as she did him.

The guard left the office without another word and closed the door behind him. The Alpha's scent surrounded her and Tasha struggled not to close her eyes and breathe deeply.

"Bryan told me that you had a family emergency and needed my help," Adam said as he gestured for her to sit.

Weak-kneed, Tasha gladly took a seat on the worn brown leather couch and clasped her hands in her lap. She should be concentrating on getting her sister back instead of her desire for a male. "Yes, Alpha. I need to talk you about my sister, Crystal."

He sat in the chair across from her and leaned forward. "I'm listening."

"I'm not sure if your father told you about my family when you took over the Pack." She was so nervous she could feel sweat bead on her forehead. She hated talking about her family and sharing the pain of her past.

She could see the sympathy in his eyes when he spoke. "Why don't you tell me?"

She took a deep breath before starting. "Five years ago, my father left our family. I'm still not sure where he went, but my mother didn't take it well. Six months after he left, she ended her existence and left Crystal with me. She was eleven."

He nodded but didn't comment. She appreciated him letting her get the story out quickly. The sooner she finished, the sooner she could once again bury her pain.

"I've tried to do the best I could, but I don't always understand what she is going through. My sister Crystal is a...non-shifter." Tasha waited for his reaction. Being a non-shifter was an embarrassment for her sister. Tasha only saw how wonderful her sibling was instead of whether she could shift or not, and even though she didn't understand, she always respected Crystal's wishes. They didn't tell many people because a lot of Pack members considered non-shifters lower class.

"Go on," he told her gently, and she didn't hear or see anything negative from him.

"Crystal's had a hard time lately with some of the kids from school. That's why I think she ran away."

"Do you have any idea where she could have gone?" he asked and Tasha just stared at him. Didn't he want to ask questions about the non-shifter part of the story? He doesn't say anything more, instead simply waiting for her reply.

"I do. I talked to her best friend and she told me that Crystal has been talking to a boy in the city over the Internet. She probably went there." Tasha spoke quickly. "I have his name and number. I keep trying to call but no one is answering. He is older and I'm worried about what he might do to her."

Adam leaned over and placed his hand over hers. "Give me the information and I will find her. I promise you that."

Tasha could feel tears threaten to fall in relief. "Thank, you Alpha. Thank you."

He squeezed her hand before releasing it. "That is what I am here for. Do you have the information with you?"

Tasha nodded and dug in her purse for her small notebook. Her hand still tingled from where Adam had touched her. "I wrote it all down." She tore out a page and handed it to him, hoping he didn't notice her hands shake.

"I'll work on this and let you know what I find out," he told her as he stood. He reached down and helped her stand. She bit back her moan when his touch caused her body once again to tingle. Her breasts felt fuller and heavy, her stomach tightened, and her sex clinched. It was unbelievable how much she could want one man.

They stood close, not quite touching, and stared at each other for several minutes. Adam shook his head and took a step back. "I'll be in touch."

Tasha turned and took a deep cleansing breath. She needed to get a hold of herself. It would be wrong to throw herself at her Alpha's feet and beg him to take her.

"Thank you," she murmured as she made her way to the door, knowing he would still be able to hear.

Hell, with wolf senses, he could do a lot more than just hear well. There was no doubt in her mind that he knew just how much she wanted him. Then again she was also a wolf shifter. His need had saturated the room.

She left the room with a small smile on her face. It felt like way too long since she'd had anything to smile about.

Adam watched as Tasha walked out of his office. His cock was throbbing from the closeness of the female, and he adjusted himself as he sat behind his desk. He typed the name Tasha had given him into his computer as he started his search for the young man who had one of his Pack members before picking up the phone trying to get a hold of him. Just like Tasha, he didn't get an answer.

Searching the Internet, he didn't find anything on him either. Having one more avenue to check, he dialled a friend. The area code for the phone number was for the city not too far away. Luckily he had friends in the area already.

"Hello?"

"Hey, man, it's Adam."

"Adam! How's it going?" Cain asked and Adam felt an instant calm. Cain always had that effect on him.

"Pretty much the same." Adam could tell Cain the truth. Cain had been in charge of the investigation of the attacks six months ago along with Adam. They'd spent a lot of time together during the long months and had become even better friends than when they were just pups. Cain was also the one person Adam had confided in when his worries about his dad seemed overwhelming. "Dad's not doing so well."

"I'm sorry," Cain said. "Is there anything I can do? Or the family? You know we'll do anything to help."

"Right now I don't know what else to do, but I'm calling for a different reason." Adam went on to explain to Cain about the runaway teenager and gave him the information on the man he was looking for.

"I'll look into the kid," he promised. "Are you coming up?"

Adam wasn't surprised by the question. With there being a good chance that Crystal was in the city,

Adam had to look for himself. It was just the way he was made. Cain knew him too well. "Yeah, I'll leave tomorrow morning and drive up," Adam told him.

"I'll go by the address and see if there's any word about the girl." Cain told him before Adam heard shuffling around and he paused. "Emily says you'll stay here if you have to spend the night in the city."

Adam couldn't keep the grin from breaking out on his face. Cain's mate was the sweetest but most stubborn female he'd ever met. She gave Cain a run for his money, keeping the Enforcer on his toes. "Tell Emily I'd be honoured."

Cain laughed then the sound of kissing travelled over the phone line.

"I'll let you go, man, and see you in the morning," Adam said a second before he heard Emily squeal and Cain's grunt goodbye.

Later, Adam closed his office door and started for his room before sensing someone on the back porch. He stopped and debated on whether or not to go out to talk to his father.

Deciding he needed to tell Christian about his trip to the city the next day, Adam turned around and headed in his father's direction. As he stepped outside into the cool night air, he saw his dad leaning against the railing of the porch. He opened his eyes as Adam walked towards him.

"Dad, how are you?"

His father's lips turned up. "I'm fine son."

Adam hadn't seen his father smile in so long that he stood for a minute and enjoyed it. "I'm surprised you're still up."

His father shrugged. "I knew you were busy but I wanted a minute of your time."

"You could have interrupted me." Adam didn't like the idea that his father had waited to talk to him. Nothing was more important than his family. He hoped his father knew that.

"I figured I'd just get some fresh air while waiting on you." When his father started to look uncomfortable, Adam remembered the older man hadn't gone back into the office since he'd heard about the attack. Maybe he should consider some changes after all. It might help Christian move on. It might help everyone in fact. "So what did you want to talk about?"

His father turned and lifted his head. "You know I've always loved our territory."

Adam did the same and inhaled, bringing in the familiar smells that were home. "As do I."

His father turned back to him and Adam was surprised by the emotion in his eyes. "I can't forget. I know you want me to be better but everything around here reminds me of my failure."

Adam opened his mouth to argue but his father hurried on.

"Yes, my failure. It might not have been my fault, but if I had done things differently, she might not have been hurt."

Adam didn't know what to say. It wasn't Christian's fault. It wasn't anyone's fault except for the madman who had committed the terrible crimes against the most innocent of them. But he knew it didn't matter how many times he told his father that. Christian wouldn't be able to move on until he forgave himself.

"Logan has invited me to his territory," his father told him, still meeting his stare.

Adam nodded. "I think that's a great idea."

His father's mouth dropped open, and he blinked several times. "You do?" he asked in a surprised tone.

Adam nodded. "For some reason, Logan can reach you. If being here bothers you, I think that a break may be in order."

"You surprise me, son." His father reached out and grasped his hands. "In a good way."

"I just want you to be happy, Dad," Adam told him, meaning every word. If he couldn't have Logan in his territory to stay with his dad, it made sense Christian should go up there. Adam couldn't believe he hadn't thought about it before. His father had not left the area since the attack. This was his chance to get away from the Pack and hopefully find some closure. Yes, the more he thought about it, the better the idea sounded.

"Thank you." He squeezed Adam's hands before releasing them.

Adam winked and grinned at his father. "Besides, that territory is on high alert since Marissa found out she was expecting. You couldn't be safer."

The sound of his father's soft chuckle made his heart swell with happiness. "That is very true, son. Now, tell me what you were working so hard on in your office."

Adam shared with him everything Tasha had told him.

"That's a good girl there. She has done everything she can to help her sister," his father commented.

"I was thinking about having Marissa talk to the girl. Maybe meeting another non-shifter and seeing how happy Marissa is will help," Adam shared.

"I think that would be perfect. Logan is driving down tomorrow to pick me up. When I get to the house, I'll talk to Gage about it."

"I'd appreciate it. I'm leaving for the city early tomorrow but give me a call after you talk to them." Adam stepped back but his father stopped him with a hand on his arm.

Then the older man embraced him. Adam held back tears as he hugged his father. Maybe, just maybe, everything was going to work out.

Chapter Two

It was still dark when Adam closed the door to the house and walked to his SUV. He threw his overnight bag into the truck, turned around and ran right into Tasha.

He reached out and steadied her as she almost fell. "What are you doing here?" he asked, his hands still clasped around her upper arms.

"I want to come with you," she told him and lifted a backpack to show him.

Adam looked from the backpack to the woman several times. "How'd you even know I would be going?"

She grinned.

He waited. Since he'd become Alpha, he'd learned patience. It didn't take more than a minute. Tasha started to fidget, shifting from foot to foot.

She rolled her eyes but answered finally. "You're hands on. There's a good chance that Crystal's in the city, so it would only make sense to check it out."

All Adam could concentrate on were the words 'hands on'. It was just a reminder of just how *hands on* he wanted to get with Tasha...which was the last thing he should be thinking about.

"I knew you'd want to go to the city yourself, so I want to come with you," she restated.

"Absolutely not." There was no way he was going to take a female and place her in any danger. Yeah, that was a good excuse.

"You need me to go with you." She tossed her head and he watched as the black silk strands swept off her shoulders.

"I need you to stay here," he argued.

Tasha frowned as she dropped her bag and fisted her hands on her hips. "Do you expect my sister to just get in the car with you because you order her to? She's a teenager, she still knows better than that."

Adam hadn't thought about that and didn't like that she had. "I'm her Alpha. If I tell her..."

Tasha laughed and the sound had his cock lengthening.

"She's also a teenager who feels lost right now. The Pack Alpha is not going to change that."

She was right. If Crystal was feeling confused enough to travel and stay with a man she didn't know, being her Alpha wasn't going to matter much. If he took Tasha, at least she would be there to help him handle the teenager.

He studied her, wondering how long they would keep playing with fire. Sooner or later, one of them was going to snap. The attraction between them was burning.

He sighed, knowing he didn't have any other choice. Plus he could use the time to talk to her about taking Crystal to see Marissa.

He picked up the bag she'd dropped. "Get in the car."

She didn't gloat. Rather, she just nodded, turned and opened the passenger door.

* * * *

Tasha let out a sigh of relief as the tall buildings of the city came into view. Sitting next to Adam and having to keep her hands to herself had been torture.

He had kept the conversation light and Tasha knew he was trying to keep her thoughts away from her sister. He'd succeeded in keeping her thoughts away from why they were going into the city because she couldn't stop staring at his hands as they gripped the steering wheel.

She fantasised about what those hands would feel like on her body. She could almost feel those strong hands spreading her legs and moving up her thighs to her bare mound.

Oh, she could imagine his skilful fingers teasing her opening as her own juices leaked out and coated his fingers. He would push those digits inside and her body would tighten.

The resulting orgasm…

"Tasha?"

Tasha's head snapped around as she realised she had drifted off. Her panties were soaked, and if *she* could smell the arousal in the small confines, she knew Adam could too.

He cleared his throat twice before he spoke. "We're here."

She knew she wasn't imaging the huskiness of his voice when he shifted in his seat, doing nothing to hide the enormous erection tenting his jeans.

Tasha tried to pull her gaze away from Adam's lap but found herself licking her lips. His low moan had her lifting her eyes to his face.

He started to lean forward and Tasha's eyes flickered closed. Their lips were only a breath apart when someone pounded on the passenger window. They jumped apart and Tasha looked over to see a tall man smiling and waving at them.

Adam groaned and unbuckled his seatbelt. "That's my friend, Cain."

Tasha unbuckled her seatbelt and the other man opened her door for her. Her arousal disappeared as heat burned her face in embarrassment. Another moment and there was no telling what Adam's friend would have seen. She'd been more than ready to throw caution to the wind and climb onto Adam's lap.

She shook her head and ignored the wide teasing grin on Cain's face. She also refused to look at Adam. It was going to be a long visit.

Adam glared at Cain but his friend only continued to bounce on the balls of his feet and grin. He could see Emily and Tony, Cain's older brother, waiting at the front of the apartment building so he placed his hand on the small of Tasha's back and led her forward.

He greeted Emily with a kiss on her cheek and shook hands with Tony. While Adam wasn't as close to him as he was Cain, he had a lot of respect for Tony—everyone did.

"I didn't know you were in town," he greeted the other man.

Tony clapped a hand on Adam's back then turned to lead the way inside as he answered. "Had a meeting earlier with the Alpha Council and our friendly government officials."

Well, that explained it. Recently, the Council had decided to come out of hiding and let the public know that shifters really do exist. The government was helping the paranormals come out to the world.

"The government?" Tasha asked.

While all shifters knew about going public, only a few knew about the help they were getting help from the government. They reached the elevator and Tony glanced at Adam before answering Tasha.

Adam nodded in approval to tell her.

"We're getting a little help with going public," he told her.

"From the government?" Tasha clarified.

The elevator doors opened and they stepped inside. "Tony here will be the face of the Packs. When it comes out to the public that shifters exist, he'll stand in front of the world and let them see we're as normal as them.

Tasha seemed to think about that, so Adam gave his attention to Cain. If he was still resting his hand on her back, no one needed to notice.

"Did you get any more information for me?" he asked Cain.

"Sure did," Cain said just as the elevator dinged and the doors opened.

They walked down a small hallway to an open door. Adam glanced at Cain but it was Emily who answered his unasked question.

"Cain was so excited to see you, he ran out the moment you pulled up," she explained.

Cain threw his arm around her shoulders and hugged her tightly. "She's kidding," he addressed the group, as Tony and Tasha laughed.

Adam's heart warmed. With the faint blush on Cain's face, he had the feeling Emily wasn't the kidder.

Adam sat next to Tasha as Cain, Emily, and Tony discussed the best way to move forward in finding Tasha's sister. Cain had been able to get an address to go along with the name and phone number. Being the Enforcer of his Pack, Cain had very good investigative skills.

He'd also found out that Mike Lawson had a minor criminal background. Mostly petty theft and some drug charges, but it was enough to reinforce that they needed to get Crystal back as soon as possible.

"No one was at the apartment last night went I went by," Cain told the group. "But when I talked to some of the neighbours, they gave me the names of a couple clubs he likes to frequent.

"Crystal's too young to get into any of the clubs here," Tasha argued.

Adam reached over and held her hand. "We'll find her."

Tasha nodded and blinked back tears.

"Why don't you guys set up a plan and I'll show Tasha to the guest room," Emily said, standing.

Cain stood also and Adam didn't miss the hand he ran down his mate's back. Cain winked at him when the girls walked out of the room.

"I have to say I never thought I'd see you like this," Adam admitted to his friend.

Cain sat back down crossed his big arms over his chest. "What's that supposed to mean?"

Adam held his hands up in a mock surrender. "Nothing, man, you just seem to be so...so..."

"Whipped!" Tony added when Adam trailed off.

Cain's eyes narrowed and Adam leaned back to get out of the line of fire. Then the big Enforcer surprised him by smiling. "Just wait," he said, still grinning. "Just wait until you meet your mates."

Tony groaned, but Adam looked towards the hallway where the women had disappeared. Was it possible? He didn't know much about mating. His mother had died when he was still young and he only had a handful of memories with her.

He didn't know if Tasha was his mate or not, but one thing was certain. He had never in his life had such strong feelings for anyone like he did Tasha.

The attraction he'd felt for women in the past paled in comparison to the hot, burning need that consumed him when Tasha was around.

He hadn't realised he'd drifted off into his own thoughts until he heard Cain and Tony laughing.

* * * *

After an unsuccessful day of searching the city for a sign of her sister, Tasha changed into a tight pair of low-rise jeans and a revealing purple cami. She hadn't brought anything to wear to go out clubbing looking for her sister. Luckily, she was about the same size as Emily, and the other woman had loaned her some clothes.

She brushed her black hair until it shined and applied more make-up than usual. Looking at herself in the mirror, she decided she didn't look too bad.

The door opened behind her, and she turned towards her Alpha. His mouth dropped open and he stared at her breasts. Excited by the attention, they stood out for him. She would have been embarrassed if he wasn't sporting an impressive erection beneath his black slacks.

Tasha looked him over as his eyes continued to bore holes into her. At just six feet tall, he was shorter than the other two men in the apartment, but to her five-foot-four frame, he was just right. He wore all black—slacks and a long-sleeved, button-down shirt. His dark brown hair fell over his forehead and her fingers itched to grab hold of it.

He must have been thinking the same, because before she knew what was happening, his long strides brought him closer and his hands found their way tangled into her hair.

"If you don't want me to kiss you, you had better tell me now," he told her in a husky voice.

Tasha couldn't deny what she wanted so she licked her lips and nodded. "I want you to."

His eyes narrowed for an instant before his mouth slammed down on hers. His tongue pushed between her lips and she gladly opened for him.

Adam immediately took control of the kiss, dominating and pulling her into an erotic dance. Their tongues stroked and played and their bodies pressed intimately together until she could feel his arousal rub against her stomach.

She moaned into his mouth while his hands moved down and cupped her bottom. Tasha pressed up against him, needing some relief for the ache of her throbbing pussy. Lifting one leg, she wrapped it around his waist and started to move. He nipped her bottom lip before sucking it into his mouth. He shifted one hand from her ass to between her legs. Her vision darkened when he pressed his thumb against her swollen clit.

Her body tightened, she was close enough to release to almost taste it. Her sex pulsed in need to be filled, and her nipples tightened into hard nubs. Pure pleasure heated her skin, then someone cleared their throat. Surprised, she jumped away from Adam.

A blush stained her face as she looked over to see Cain standing in the open doorway.

She'd practically humped herself to orgasm on her Alpha. Never in her life had she acted so wantonly and slutty. Plus, she was frustrated, needy, and confused. She peeked at Adam.

He didn't look much better as he panted and adjusted himself. "You have the worst timing," he complained to the other man.

"Sorry," Cain told them, but the grin on his face didn't match his words. "We're all ready and waiting in the living room, but if you two need a couple of minutes..."

Adam growled at his friend and Tasha looked up at him. His eyes were glowing but he seemed to be gaining control over his body. "No, we're ready."

He offered his hand to Tasha and she took it as he led her out of the room.

No one said anything as they went meet by the front door, went downstairs and got in the cars, but they would have been able to smell what had been going on.

Embarrassed as she was, she was also disappointed that they'd been interrupted.

Adam winced as the loud music assaulted his ears. This was the third club they'd visited and he was getting tired of the crowds and music.

There hadn't been a sign of the girl. The group had split up to hit all of the clubs on the list. This club was the last one on his and Tasha's list. He'd spoken to Cain and Tony, and they weren't having any better luck. Cain had refused to let Emily come with them on the search, and to Adam's surprise, she'd agreed. Maybe the two of them were getting the mating thing down.

Tasha pointed to the back of the club, and with a heavy sigh, he nodded. They circled the club, looking for the teenager. When they almost reached the back corner, Tasha grabbed his sleeve and tugged.

"She's here!"

Adam took in the men who sat, surrounding the girl, at the table. The female had her elbows on the table, looking miserable.

"I can get her out of her, but if they fight me, it can turn ugly." He pulled Tasha close to speak in her ear. "I'm going to call Cain and Tony. Stay over by the wall and keep an eye on her."

Tasha nodded and moved to the back wall. It would give her a good view of the table but keep her out of their sight.

Adam went out front and made the call before returning to Tasha. She was still in the same spot, trying to keep an eye on her sister while a large bald man in leather was hitting on her. Adam felt a growl start deep in his chest and clenched his fists, trying to control his temper. Pushing through the crowd, he walked up to the two and leaned close to Tasha and pressed his body into hers.

"Hey, baby," he said loud enough for the other man to hear.

Playing along, Tasha rubbed her body against his and ran her hands over his chest. "What took you so long?"

Crissy Smith

Adam brushed his hand over the low-cut top she wore, feeling her hard nipples. Then he looked over at the other man. "Can I help you?"

The big man shook his head and walked away. Tasha leaned into Adam and laughed. "I think you scared him."

Adam nipped her ear. "Good. Now keep an eye on your sister."

Tasha nodded and Adam moved his body more securely in front of hers, giving her just enough room to turn her head and watch the teenager.

A savage need to mark the woman in his arms almost overtook his body. He didn't know if it was the call of a mate, but every instinct inside him screamed to make Tasha his. And only his. Adam fought the instinct but didn't think it would hurt if others knew she was taken. He started at her chin and ran his tongue up to her ear. Tasha shivered but didn't take her eyes off her sister.

Sucking her lobe into his mouth, he nibbled the soft skin. She moaned and pressed against him.

"Your skin's so soft. I'd like to mark with my mouth, with my hands, my body," he whispered.

Her gaze still on the table, Tasha moved her hands down his chest to where he was straining against his zipper. She moved them up and down before squeezing him.

Adam thrust into her hand and latched his mouth onto the side of her neck. His cock was hard enough to pound nails and, after being interrupted earlier, was practically begging to be released.

Knowing that if she continued to touch him he would lose it, Adam captured Tasha's wrists and moved them up over her head. She moaned again arching her body to him.

204

When her eyes started to flicker closed, he teased his tongue on the shell of her ear before whispering, "Keep your eyes open."

"Ugh," she complained but complied.

Pleased, Adam moved his mouth from her ear downward, licking and sucking her skin.

A prickle of awareness invaded and told him Cain and Tony had arrived. Pulling away from Tasha, he grabbed her chin. "We *will* finish this."

Her dark eyes lit up and she licked her lips. "Promises. Promises."

Catching Cain's gaze, Adam nodded to the table. Cain and Tony moved from the front door in that direction, and Adam grabbed Tasha's arms and held her close as they walked to the table.

They all approached the table at the same time.

"Tasha!" the young girl greeted, surprised.

The rest of the table turned towards them.

"Let's go, Crystal. I'm taking you home," Tasha told her sternly.

Adam didn't miss the look of relief that flashed over the teenager's face as she stood. Before she could move away from the table, the man on her left grabbed her wrist.

"We're not done partying, honey. Sit back down." He yanked and the girl fell into his lap.

Adam growled, but before he could react, Tony leaned closer to the table. "Let the girl go." When the man laughed, Tony glanced over his shoulder. "You see those two men over there."

Everyone looked, and indeed, there were two large tattooed men only a few feet away.

"Those are the bouncers of the bar. Now, while they won't appreciate you bringing in an underage girl, they probably won't kill you." Tony straightened and raised his voice to make certain everyone around the table could hear the rest. "These two?" He motioned to Adam and Cain. "I can't make that promise."

The man let go of Crystal and she scrambled into Tasha's arms. Adam nodded to Tony, knowing he would take care of the situation, and ushered the two females out of the bar.

Crystal cried in her sister's arms while telling them how sorry she was.

Chapter Three

Adam watched Tasha hold her sister while the girl cried. They were back at Cain's where they'd taken Crystal into one of the guestrooms.

"I'm sorry." Crystal sobbed. "I just wanted to see what it would be like outside of the Pack."

Tasha patted her back and kept her voice calm. "I know, honey. But you can never do that again. You were very lucky that nothing bad had happened."

"I know! But after I got to the city, I was too scared to call you," Crystal explained.

"You can always call me," Tasha assured her sister and Adam felt his heart break at everything the two females had to face.

The teenager looked up at him and blushed. "I'm sorry, Alpha. I know I have to be punished, but please don't blame Tasha."

Adam clasped his hands behind his back and walked to the side of the bed. "You could have been seriously injured or worse." He shook his head in disappointment and Crystal dropped her gaze.

"But I think you've been punished enough," he told her and her gaze met his again. "However, I do want you to talk to a friend of mine."

The girl made a face and rubbed her eyes. "I don't need to see a shrink."

Adam chuckled. "This woman isn't a shrink. She's the mate to an Alpha who happens to be a very good friend of mine."

The girl looked confused but nodded. "Okay."

Adam smiled at her and crouched of the bed so they could be eye to eye without her straining her neck. "I think you two have a lot in common. You'll be able to talk to her about things you don't anyone else."

"What things?" she asked suspiciously.

"Marissa is also a non-shifter."

Crystal's eyes widened and her mouth dropped open. "She's a non-shifter and she mated with an Alpha?"

Adam stood, knowing he gave the girl enough to think about to keep her from running again. "She is. Her childhood was pretty rough, but I'll let her tell you about that. The important thing is that you can tell her how you feel and she'll understand." He met Tasha's eyes and smiled. "Now I'll let you two get some sleep. We have a long drive tomorrow."

Adam started out of the room but Crystal's voice stopped him. "Thank you, Alpha."

He turned and winked at her. "You're welcome."

She was giggling as he closed the door.

Adam walked down the hall to the living room and stopped in the doorway. Emily was straddling Cain's lap and the two were involved in a deep, sensual kiss. He grinned and walked farther into the room. Not only was the couch his bed for the night, but Cain was having too much fun. It seemed a little payback was in order.

"I'm not interrupting, am I?" he teased.

The two broke apart and Cain groaned. "I guess I deserve this."

Emily moved off his lap but Cain kept an arm around her, holding her close to his side.

"Yes, you do." Adam told him and shared a smile with Emily. She laughed and poked Cain in the ribs.

"Karma, baby," she taunted her mate

Cain's laugh filled the room and Adam relaxed, feeling the stress of the last couple days start to leave his body.

He'd been there as Cain struggled with his intense feelings for his mate. He was relieved to find that Cain and Emily seemed peaceful in the relationship. It gave him hope for his own future. One he was sure would include Tasha.

* * * *

With a kiss from Emily and a handshake from Cain, Adam said goodbye and started the long drive to Gage Wolf's territory. It was the first time he would enter another Alpha's territory as an Alpha himself. He knew things would be a little different. As an Alpha, he would be given respect and placed above others. Adam still wasn't used to that.

Lost in his thoughts, he jolted when Tasha gripped his arm.

"Sorry." She quickly let go.

Adam cursed himself and sent her a smile. "No, I'm sorry. I was just thinking about Gage's territory," he told her, not wanting her to think he didn't like her touch.

"That's where your father is, right?" she asked, keeping her voice low.

Adam looked in the rear-view mirror and saw that Crystal was asleep. He relaxed his grip on the steering wheel and glanced quickly at Tasha. He wondered what the other Pack members thought about his family. While everyone seemed to take his transition to Alpha rather well, he didn't want to take it for granted.

"Yes, he's visiting his old friend there," Adam explained.

"Logan?" she asked.

Adam nodded. "My father and Logan have been friends a long time. Years ago, they were both Enforcers in their Packs so they worked together and became friends."

"It's good for him to have friends." Tasha touched his arm again. "He'll be okay."

Adam glanced in the rear-view mirror again before he spoke. "I don't know."

Tasha started to move her hand up and down his arm. While he was sure she meant it as a comforting gesture, it was doing more powerful things to his body. And he didn't want her to stop.

"I do. Your father was a great Alpha. A man of compassion. He'll come through this. He was right to turn the Pack over to you and give himself a chance at something else," Tasha said, and the sincerity in her voice squeezed at his heart.

"Thank you." He told her and meant it more than anything.

She moved her hand down and linked her fingers with his before settling in her seat and closing her eyes.

The tension that had built while he spoke about his father started to drain as they sat in silence. It was nice—the opportunity to sit quietly with someone. While it seemed people at home constantly surrounded him as the Alpha, he could get used to finding solace in Tasha's company.

He didn't know if that was even possible, but to find out, he had to try. He was certain Tasha was his mate. He needed her calming influence almost as much as he wanted her.

And oh, how he wanted her.

His cock hadn't gone down from half-mast since she'd walked into his office a few days earlier. It didn't matter how many times he jacked off. He was unfulfilled. If he didn't get to taste her sweet body soon, he would have to go for a run. His wolf needed to be let out.

Not only did he need the physical release but he needed to take care of the animal inside who was scratching to be let out. His wolf didn't understand why he wasn't taking care of his needs. Sometimes it was easier to just let the animal be in control.

Then again that was why he needed his mate—to keep him human.

Tasha fell asleep as they reached the last leg of their travel. Adam kept her hand in his, enjoying the small contact.

A short time later, Adam turned onto the paved road that would lead him to the gates to enter Gage's territory. He reached over and ran a hand over Tasha's face. She moaned as she opened her eyes and straightened in her seat.

"We're almost there," he told her.

She rubbed the sleep from her eyes before reaching back and shaking her sister awake. "Crystal. Wake up, honey, we're there."

The teenager sat up and stretched.

Adam watched through the rear-view mirror as the young girl took a look around. He was pleased he was able to give Crystal the chance to meet Marissa. Hopefully she would be able to see how wonderful her life could be. The large iron gates came into view and Adam slowed his speed.

"It's so big!" Crystal commented from the back seat.

Adam laughed at the girl's excitement. "Yes. Gage has one of the most beautiful territories."

Tasha shook her head while she stared out the passenger window. "Ours is perfect."

"Yes, it is," he agreed.

Adam stopped at the gate and rolled down his window. A young man, no more than twenty, stepped up to the car.

"Hi. Can I help you?" he greeted.

"Yes, I'm Adam White. I believe Gage is expecting us," Adam told him.

The guard smiled and waved to another to let them in. "Yes, Alpha. Gage said to drive right up to the main house."

"Thank you." Adam nodded to the guard.

The man stepped back and Adam drove through the gate and up the drive. As he pulled in front of the main house, the front door opened. Gage, Marissa, Logan, and Adam's father stepped out and approached the vehicle.

Adam opened his door as Gage opened Tasha's and Logan opened Crystal's. After closing the car door, Adam found himself wrapped in his father's arms and lifted off his feet in a strong hug.

Once he was released, Adam looked closely at his father. "You look great." And he did.

"I *feel* great," his father said, a huge smile on his face.

Adam threw his arm around his father and the two of them walked in front of the car where the others waited.

"I'm glad you made it safely," Gage stated, offering him a hand.

Adam accepted it and bowed his head to the older Alpha. "Thank you for inviting us into your territory."

Gage gave his hand a squeeze before letting go and stepping aside so his mate could greet Adam. Adam bent his head and accepted a kiss on the cheek from the beautifully pregnant woman.

"Welcome, Alpha Adam," she said softly.

"Thank you." Adam replied trying to hide the jolt of surprise from being called Alpha. It still felt made him feel uneasy sometimes. Especially in front of such a great Alpha like Gage.

Logan stood next to Gage, and pushing his uncomfortable feelings aside, Adam walked up to his father's friend. Instead of shaking his hand, he gave the other man a brief hug and whispered, "Thank you."

Logan patted his back. "You're welcome."

Noticing Tasha and Crystal off to the side, Adam motioned them closer. Tasha walked confidently up to him but Crystal lingered behind.

"Let me introduce you all to two of my favourite Pack members, Tasha and Crystal," Adam said to the group, hoping they would make an extra effort to make the women feel welcomed.

Marissa, like a true Alpha's mate, embraced Crystal and held the girl tightly. "I am so glad you're okay, Crystal. Everyone was so worried about you."

Once Marissa had released her, Crystal dropped her head. "I'm sorry for all the trouble I caused." She spoke barely above a whisper.

With her arm still around the teenager, Marissa hushed her. "That's all over now. If I told you how many times I ran away from my Pack—"

"Marissa," Gage warned in a low voice.

Crystal moved closer to Marissa, and Tasha moved closer to Adam. He knew how scary Gage could be in Alpha mode, but he was also one of the most honourable men Adam had ever met. He wrapped his arm around Tasha's waist while Marissa waved a hand in the air at Gage.

"Oh, stop scaring her." Then she whispered to Crystal, "He thinks he is big and bad, but you should see him reading all the baby books."

"Marissa!" Gage snapped at her.

Pulling the girl towards the door, she only laughed. "I'm just saying that maybe you should calm down before you give yourself a stroke. I wasn't going to tell her *everything*."

Gage growled before following her into the house.

Adam held back his laugh until the three disappeared from sight. Then he wasn't the only one laughing. Logan and his father were joining him. Wiping a tear from his eye, he looked over at his father and watched the man who had been so depressed grin.

"I can hear you three yokels," Gage hollered from the house.

Logan sobered and pointed towards the house. "We should go in before he comes out to get us. Marissa doesn't allow any roughhousing inside."

"Logan!" Gage yelled.

Biting his lip to keep his amusement inside, Adam led Tasha up the stairs.

* * * *

Adam stepped out of the bathroom into the guestroom with a towel wrapped around his waist. Marissa had whisked Crystal away to another room so Gage had taken Adam and Tasha to their rooms to clean up or rest—whatever they preferred.

Adam wanted to spend some time with his father but a shower had sounded great. Now clean and energised, he looked forward to going downstairs for a stiff drink and good conversation.

At the knock at his door, Adam turned and strolled to it. Pulling it open, he expected his father but found Tasha outside his door instead. Her eyes widened before dropping to his waist, reminding him he wasn't dressed. Before he could speak, she licked her lips and his cock jumped beneath the material.

"Tasha," he practically moaned. He wasn't sure how long he was going to be able to keep his hands off her if she didn't leave quickly.

She lifted her hand and ran a finger over the small scar beneath his nipple he'd gotten as a child. This time he did moan and caught her hand in his.

"If you come inside, we won't be talking," he warned.

Her gaze met his and she smiled. "I hope not."

Then she was pushing him back into his room and closed the door. Adam stood stunned as she sent a seductive grin before reaching for the hem of her shirt and pulling it over her head.

"I have too many clothes on," she announced.

His throat had gone dry so all Adam could do was nod. Tasha ran her slender fingers over the waistband of her pants before pushing them down her hips. When she straightened, she only wore a matching pair of blue panties and bra.

"God, you're beautiful." Adam finally managed to speak.

She tossed her hair and laughed. "I could say the same about you. You have a gorgeous body, Alpha."

Her use of his title had Adam's body cooling. In the past, women of the Pack would offer themselves to the leader as a gift. No Pack he knew of still had that practice, but he needed to make sure Tasha didn't think she had to give him her body.

"You don't have to do this," he told her even as regret coursed through his body.

She took several steps. "Oh yes, I do."

Adam backed away as she continued towards him. "No, you don't. I don't expect anything from you."

She stopped and a thoughtful look crossed her face. Then she laughed. "Do you think I'm only sleeping with you because you're my Alpha?"

"I just want to make sure you know that being with me is your choice," he told her honestly. He wanted nothing more to than to take her and bury himself as deep inside as possible, but he wouldn't take it as a 'thank you' for finding her sister. He wanted Tasha to be with him because she just couldn't stand not having him any longer. He needed her to want him as much as he wanted her.

She'd reached him when his legs hit the bed, stopping his retreat. "I see. Now how can I prove this is something that I want?"

Her eyes sparkled with mischief when he met them.

"Oh, I know!" she said before dropping to her knees in front of him.

She yanked the towel off and hummed her approval. "I see that no matter what you say there is a part of you that wants me."

"All of me wants you," he assured her. "All of you."

With a firm grip, she wrapped her hand around his leaking cock. "I'm glad to hear that," she said, right before engulfing him.

Adam moaned and buried his hands in her hair and she started a strong sucking rhythm. The wet moist heat that surrounded and teased his cock was almost too much. She used her tongue to massage the sensitive spot directly under the mushroomed head. Unable to remain still, he bucked against her mouth. "Yes!"

Tasha made a sound at the back of her throat, sending vibrations through his cock to the rest of his body. Not wanting to come before he was inside her, Adam yanked on her hair and pulled her away from him.

Still on her knees, she gazed up at him. The sight of her before him was almost too perfect and he could barely keep from shooting his seed. He helped her stand with a hand on her arm and turned her until she was bent over the bed.

Adam rubbed and teased her bottom before pulling her panties down her legs. She was already wet when he briefly teased her folds. Her scent flooded all of his senses. There was no doubt that she wanted him, that she was already ready. His fingers slipped inside her pussy and she moaned lowly.

Adam wanted every sound he could pull from her, wanted to hear her beg. He pumped two fingers in and out of her sex. She lifted her hips and pushed

Crissy Smith

back, drawing his digits even deeper. Each time she pushed back, Adam twisted his fingers, driving them in and making her cry out in ecstasy. Almost desperately, she rode his fingers and he knew it was almost time. He pulled his fingers from her body and replaced them with the tip of his cock.

"Please, Adam!" she begged. "I want you."

Adam rubbed his cock against her pussy, causing a low moan to escape both of them. With shaky hands, he reached around and cupped her breasts through the silk that still covered them. He licked up her spine until he caught the back of her bra in his teeth and ripped the fabric apart.

"Oh!" Tasha cried as he removed the ruined lingerie from her.

"Now enough with the talking," he said, squeezing her.

Tasha pushed back against him, silently telling him what she wanted. With one hand playing and pulling on one pert nipple, he moved the other down to play with her clit.

She shamelessly rubbed against him, trying to get enough pressure to go over the edge. Catching her ear lobe between his teeth, he slid both hands along her body to grip her hips. He bit down as he plunged inside. Tasha cried out as he went all the way with his first thrust. Licking the small bite, he pulled out and slammed back inside.

Tasha wasn't a passive lover. She moved into each stroke and met him in every way. Her hot body accepted and milked him each time he withdrew and entered again. Adam felt her body tighten only seconds before she dropped her head and screamed into the bed.

Three more thrusts and Adam was there with her, howling his climax.

Chapter Four

Adam stroked Tasha's back as her head rested on his chest and she slept. After another round of mind-blowing sex, they had settled into his bed where he had been happy to hold her.

Her breath whispered across his skin and his body came back to life. Easing out from under her, Adam pulled on a pair of jeans before quietly leaving the room. He knew he'd missed his chance of visiting with his dad since the house was silent as he made his way through it. Knowing where he would find the kitchen from his previous visits, he walked down the hall with thoughts of Tasha in his head.

She was one of the strongest, most confident women he'd ever met. To him, she was absolutely perfect. She was the kind of woman a man would be lucky to have and would make a wonderful mate to an Alpha.

Adam paused at the entrance to the kitchen and shook his head. A mate to an Alpha? Where had that thought come from? Hoping to shove the thought to the back of his mind since he didn't want to think about it, he pushed the door open to the kitchen.

He blinked at the bright light, surprised to find it still on. Then he saw Gage sitting at the kitchen table with a beer in front of him.

Gage looked up and nodded to the nearly empty bottle in front of him. Adam smiled and went to the fridge. He pulled out two and walked over to the table. Taking a seat, he handed the extra beer to Gage.

"How are things going?" Gage asked with a wide smile.

Adam knew the other man could smell Tasha all over him so he didn't pretend otherwise. "Pretty damn good," he answered.

Gage nodded and took a long pull from the bottle. "A woman will do that."

Adam sighed, thinking about Tasha again. It would be so easy to get used to having her around.

As if he could read Adam's mind, Gage laughed before saying, "There's no use fighting it. She buried herself inside you until she is all you think about."

Adam tipped the beer back and drank.

"Trust me on this," Gage continued.

"I'm her Alpha." Adam shared his fear for the first time.

"And you're worried that she only wanted to be with you because of that?" Gage asked, amusement thick in his voice.

"No, I'm worried that, when she doesn't want me anymore, she will stay because of it," Adam told him.

"Ah I see." Gage stretched his arms over his head. "I take it you haven't been with a Pack member since you've become Alpha."

Adam didn't answer. He didn't need to.

"Women are tricky creatures. Marissa had it in her head she was going to leave even after we became mates."

Adam looked up, surprised. He hadn't known that. "How'd you make her stay?"

Gage shook his head. "I didn't. She knew her place was with me. Her head and her heart just couldn't agree."

The conversation wasn't making Adam feel any better. "Tasha and Crystal have already had a rough go at it. I'd hate to cause them anymore pain."

"Who says you'll cause them pain?" the other Alpha asked thoughtfully. "Maybe it's you she's been waiting on to take the pain away."

Adam leaned back and brought his drink up to his lips but paused. "I hadn't thought of it that way."

"You'll make a good Alpha. You're kind and caring but strong. All you have to do is believe in yourself." Gage met his gaze.

"I have some big shoes to fill," Adam admitted.

"Yes, I know. I've been there. And, like me, you already have a big supporter in your corner. Your father wouldn't have left the Pack to you if you weren't ready. Son or not."

Adam knew he was right. Cain had said something similar when Adam had first taken over. "I worry about him. I wanted to talk to him earlier but..." Adam trailed off, knowing Gage already had an idea of what had kept him.

"I wouldn't worry about that. You'll have plenty of time to talk tomorrow," Gage told him and stood. "I better get upstairs before Marissa wakes up and find me gone."

Adam smiled and tilted his bottle in a salute. "Thanks." He was thanking Gage for more than the beer, and hoped the other Alpha realised that.

"Anytime. But may I suggest you get back up before your woman wonders where you disappeared to?"

Feeling his cock stir at the thought of Tasha in his bed, Adam stood. "Good idea."

Tasha woke up with a hard, warm body pressed up against her back. With a small smile, she snuggled back, feeling Adam's morning erection dig into her bottom.

Moving her hips in a slow side-to-side motion, she was treated to Adam's arm wrapping around her and pulling her tighter against him.

"Good morning, baby," he whispered huskily next to her ear.

Her heart swelled at the endearment—one she had never been called before. "Morning."

He started thrusting his hips against her so she reached around and took a hold of him. With her thumb, she teased the slit of his cock, releasing a small pearl of liquid.

"Oh God, you have such great hands," he told her, rolling her onto her back and taking possession of her mouth.

Their tongues duelled, caressing, as his body covered hers. Already ready for him, she wrapped her legs around his waist. Adam shifted and kissed down her neck until he reached her breasts. Tasha arched her back when he took one hard nipple into his mouth and sucked. He nipped at it and moved and did the same to the other.

"I love your breasts. So full and soft," he whispered against her skin.

Tasha had always hated how big they were. They had been a cause of teasing as she'd gotten older and filled out before the other girls. But, with Adam worshipping them in the most loving way, for the first time she was proud of them.

Adam started to move down her body once again. She grabbed his hair, trying to pull him back up, but he just chuckled and drove his tongue into her belly button.

Tasha had never thought that was an erotic zone, but with him lavishing it with care, she found herself bucking under him. By the time he reached her most private of areas, she was ready to scream at him to take her. Then his skilled fingers separated her wet folds and he pushed one digit inside.

"Oh!" She panted as he pumped in and out. She lifted her hips to give him better access and he inserted a second finger. Tasha rode his hand until his mouth covered her swollen clit and he sucked.

She exploded, crying out his name. Breathing laboured, she tried to speak, but he was once again making his way up her body, leaving a trail of moisture from his tongue and her own juices.

When he covered her and bent his head, he shared her unique taste before starting to push that wonderfully long cock inside. Tasha planted her feet on the bed and lifted her hips to help him inside. In one hard, deep thrust, he entered her.

Her muscles tightened and gripped at him. He was longer than any other man she'd been with, but he fit perfectly in the most intimate way. While he slammed inside her, Tasha scratched at his shoulders. He pounded into her with a rhythm so fast a normal man could never reach it. Before she knew it, she was once again riding out another wave of ecstasy.

He grabbed her legs and moved them over his shoulders. His strokes grew desperate. Three, four, five more times he rammed into her then exploded, his deep voice echoing around the room.

As he collapsed on her, Tasha ran her hands through his hair, wanting to hold on to every second she had with this very special man. In the short time they'd been together, Adam had made her feel better than anyone else in her life. His concern for her sister was only a small part of why she admired him.

She had never felt comfortable in the company of a lot of people. She had always been a loner. It was easier to hide her and her family's problems that way. But when she was with Adam, he had the ability to draw her from her shell. First, in the city, and now, in another Pack's territory.

Try as she might, she couldn't keep her mind from moving into the future and taunting her with pictures of her and Adam together...in a more permanent situation.

She held him tighter. She knew she could never be the mate to the Alpha. She wasn't pretty or smart and she didn't have the right connections. She was just a lost woman with the responsibilities of raising a child.

Adam didn't need that kind of pressure. He had enough on his shoulders without taking care of her problems too. She blinked back tears. She'd have to let him go once they left to return home. So right now she would hang on as long as she could.

* * * *

Adam led Tasha to the living room with a hand on the small of her back. He was making no secret that the two of them had been together the night before and that morning. The house was full of wolf shifters. It would be more than obvious by their scents mixing so strongly. Secretly, she liked the possessive side of the Alpha that had appeared. It was like he was staking his claim for everyone to know who she belonged to. It felt great.

When she'd tried to sneak out of his room to get ready for the day, he had picked her up and carried her into his shower. There he had washed every inch of her body before licking the water away. In all her life, she had never felt so cherished and loved.

As she entered the large room, she saw her sister curled up on the end of the brown leather couch. Her head was bent as she leaned over and whispered to Marissa. Adam made his way to the other side of his room where his father stood.

When she saw Tasha, Crystal jumped up and ran to her, throwing her arms around her neck. "Did you know that when Marissa was my age she got kicked out of a Pack for being a non-shifter? And that she ran to the city too? She didn't even know that a non-shifter could mate with a shifter and have babies!"

Shocked by the information coming quickly from her sister, Tasha cut her gaze to the other woman. Marissa only smiled and Tasha knew her sister was in great hands.

"I didn't know that," she answered the teenager.

Crystal held onto her hand and tugged her towards the couch. "And it wasn't until she came here for her sister's mating ceremony and met Gage that she learned the truth. She had been living all by herself without any Pack for years."

Tasha took a seat next to Crystal and tried to digest all the information that her sister was telling her. To be without a Pack left a female in danger. Not only from humans but also from any Rogue wolf. She'd never heard of a *female* going Rogue.

Most Rogue shifters had either been kicked out of a Pack or left because they hadn't received the position they thought they deserved. They could be very dangerous. They didn't hold to the same standards and rules most wolves kept.

"That must have been terrible," Tasha said sympathetically to the woman.

Marissa laughed and waved a hand in the air. "Oh, it was. But if I had to do it again to make my way here to Gage, I would."

Tasha believed her as she watched Marissa run a hand over the bump in her stomach. She wondered what it would be like to have life growing inside her. To bond with a child before they were born into the world.

She found herself stroking her sister's back silently, questioning if she would be a loving mother like Marissa seemed to be, or would her genetics stop her? Would she desert her own offspring, just like her parents had?

Blinking back tears, she looked up and met Adam's eyes as he watched her. He must have sensed something wasn't right because he took a step towards her. She quickly shook her head, not wanting him to leave his father because of some silly thought she'd had. He sent her a sideways smile and turned back to his dad and Logan again.

Tasha gave her attention back to the two females in the room, not missing the fact that Marissa had also been watching her. Her sister went on to tell Tasha about how Marissa'd had a lot of the same feelings as she did. And that she could also feel the wolf inside her at times.

"Wait!" Tasha interrupted. "You never told me you could feel your wolf."

Crystal dropped her eyes and Tasha quickly looked over to Marissa.

Marissa shifted so she could place her hand on Crystal's arm.

"I never told my older sister either," Marissa explained. "I didn't know how."

Crystal looked up and tears shined in her eyes. Tasha threw her arms around the girl's shoulder and hugged her tightly. "You can tell me anything, sweetheart. But I understand that you were scared."

"I didn't know what was wrong with me. I know I can't shift, so shouldn't that mean that I don't have a wolf inside me?"

Tasha shook her head, not knowing the answer.

"But now I know that I do have the wolf inside. She's trapped on the inside just like I am on the outside." Crystal's eyes cleared and Tasha could see the excitement. "Marissa runs with Gage."

A laugh had Tasha looking up at Marissa, who clarified, "Well, obviously not *now*, but before."

Crystal laughed too and Tasha couldn't help but smile. "Well, she would run in human form. She can run faster than a normal human. I think that's because of the wolf inside. By running she's letting her wolf out a little."

Tasha nodded because it did make sense.

"So I want to try that. I want to run with the wolves!" Tasha announced loudly.

Adam's head snapped around and he walked towards them.

"You want you run with the wolves?" he asked, sounding as surprised as Tasha felt.

Crystal nodded. "Marissa said I have to start up slow. Just run a little and I can work up to a mile and then more."

Adam caught Tasha's eye and she shrugged. She didn't know what to say. So much was happening, she was feeling a little bit lost.

Crouching down in front of them, Adam took Tasha's hand, then Crystal's "How about if you start going for a run with me and your sister? That way we can keep an eye on you if you get tired."

Crystal let out a cry and threw her arms around him. "Thank you! Thank you!"

He hugged the girl back and looked over at Tasha. She wanted to kiss him right there in front of everyone. Instead, she bowed her head in gratefulness.

Later, Tasha couldn't believe she was going on a run with her Alpha and her sister. The plan was for her and Adam to change forms and run. Marissa and Gage would bring Crystal to meet them after an hour.

As she walked with Adam to the secluded spot Gage had told them about, her stomach fluttered with butterflies. It wasn't just the thought of her sister running with her for the first time that had her so nervous, but knowing Adam would be right beside her the entire time.

Going for a run as wolves was a very intimate part of being a shifter. Never before had she had the opportunity to run without a full Pack.

Adam held her hand until they reached their destination. He turned towards her and brought her hand up to his mouth. He kissed the back before turning it over and nipping her wrist.

"I can sense your uneasiness," he said gently. "And I know it's not only about your sister."

Tasha couldn't deny his words so she dropped her head. He caressed her chin before he lifted it. "Talk to me," he ordered softly.

"I've never run with a male before," she told him, her eyes darting around.

His soft laughter floated around her as he bent his head to her. "I'm glad to hear it."

She didn't look at him when she continued. "This is new for me. The feelings I have for you. We've only been together a few days and I can't..." She trailed off, not knowing what else to say.

He surprised her by yanking her to him and slamming his mouth down on hers. After the long, sensual kiss, he pulled away, panting. "I understand that this is happening fast between us, but it feels right," he told her.

Tasha nodded. It *did* feel right.

"Now, let's change so we can run. If I look at you much longer, I won't be able to resist taking you right here."

Tasha could feel a blush work up her neck to her face. She never thought she would be someone who enjoyed such strong and direct sexual talk but the intensity of his tone told her Adam wasn't joking. And that turned her on.

Chapter Five

The wind carried Tasha's body as she leapt over a fallen log and landed flawlessly next to Adam. In wolf form, Adam was huge. A perfect blend of muscle and power covered in a thick, black pelt. Her smaller body ran hard to keep up with his long strides. She felt free running beside him.

He nipped her shoulder and turned her to the east, no doubt leading her back to the spot where her sister would be waiting.

A selfish part of her wanted to continue to run with him and be alone together. She scolded herself and told her to think about her sister, but she couldn't help it. Adam was unlike any other man she'd ever been with. Watching him from afar had been one thing, but now that she knew what he tasted like and how he felt inside her, she didn't know how she was ever going to let him go.

If he weren't Pack Alpha, she would demand he mate with her and forever seal their bond. But deep down inside, she knew she was in no way right to be mated with the Alpha.

Mood suddenly changing, Tasha tucked her head and picked up speed. Just because she couldn't keep Adam didn't mean she was going to waste the time she had with him now.

As they raced back towards the house, the freedom of the running lifted her spirits. Adam led the way to the meeting spot and she only slowed down when she caught the scent of her sister.

All her senses were heightened. She could practically taste her sister's excitement mixed with nerves as they drew closer. Adam stopped running several feet away from the group so she followed suit. Soon, they stood among the three who were in human form.

Crystal walked slowly to Tasha and ran a hand through the fur that covered her neck. Tasha leaned against her sister, letting her know she enjoyed the touch.

The teenager let out a cry of delight and dropped to her knees, throwing her arms around her. It was only then that Tasha realised that she had never taken her other form around her sister. She's always been so careful not to rub in the fact that Crystal couldn't shift. Adam nuzzled her from the other side and she felt truly loved in that moment.

They waited until Crystal stood taking a deep breath before starting to run before they took off after her. Adam kept a slow pace behind Crystal so Tasha took up running beside her. Crystal's breathing came hard as she ran through the thick grass deep into the woods.

Tasha was trying to come up with a way to stop her when Adam raced in front of them and blocking their way. Almost in perfect order, Crystal and Tasha stopped next to him. The young girl was bent at the waist with her hands on her knees, drawing long gulps of air. When she looked up and over at Tasha, the smile on Crystal's face made Tasha's heart sing.

This was something they could share, to bring them closer. Instead of hiding a part of herself from Crystal, Tasha would be able to have a way for the two of them to connect. It was a precious gift.

Adam watched as Tasha, back in human form, led her younger sibling away for some quiet time. They needed to talk and there was no better time than after the run and great dinner they had shared.

Adam glanced at the watch on his wrist. His father had looked preoccupied during dinner and Adam wanted to catch up with him before it got too late again. That and he had plans for Tasha later.

Chuckling to himself, he quickly made his way to his father's room. Instead of knocking, he walked into the bedroom like he'd always done and found a sight that shocked him to the core.

His father had his arms locked around Logan as they shared a deep, intimate kiss. The two broke away when Adam entered but not before he'd seen the truth.

"Adam, close the door," his father told him quietly.

He would have loved to but the shock and confusion that clouded his mind kept him from moving.

"Adam!" his father snapped, and like a curtain lifting, his vision cleared.

There was his father, the greatest man he had ever known, standing shoulder to shoulder with another man, who was obviously his lover.

There was no doubt in his mind that they were lovers. Logan's scent was all over his father's room.

All over his father. This hadn't been a one-time incident.

And why had he never noticed that before? Sure, he had been busy but something like his dad taking a lover should have been extremely obvious. That could only mean that his father had taken great pains to ensure Adam didn't find out.

Christian took a step forward and Adam panicked.

"Stay back!" he ordered. He didn't know why he felt so hurt, so betrayed, but that was what he was feeling.

"Close the door and we'll talk about this," his father assured him calmly.

"Talk? You want to talk about this?" he questioned, his voice rising above his normal tone.

"Yes, talk. Like adults, which the three of us are."

He jerked, feeling like he'd just been slapped. His father was reprimanding *him*?

"Yes, we are adults." The cool calm voice couldn't have come from his mouth. Not with the way his body shook. "Although it doesn't look to me like the two of you do much talking."

His father didn't pull his gaze from his. "I was going to explain…"

Adam barked out a bitter laugh. "Explain? Why would you need to explain anything to me? Keeping Logan here as your little dark secret is your own business."

Christian's eyes flashed. "You will not disrespect him." His voice rose also.

Adam turned on his heel and headed out the door. "I don't have to respect him either." With the last word, he slammed the door behind him and headed towards the back of the house.

It was a good thing no one was around since he was likely to bite the head off any person who stood between him and his freedom, because the only thing he was sure of was the fact he had to get out of the house.

His long, angry strides ate up the distance until he stood once again at the edge of the woods. He quickly tore off his clothes and knelt, calling to his brother wolf. With a cry of anguish, he let the magic sweep over his body and, for the second time of the day, changed into his other form.

The wolf wanted to run. To get away from the worry, the doubt, the pain that he felt. Without someone else slowing him down, he started to run. And ran as hard and fast as he could.

He must have run for over an hour. He had enough sense to stay within the Pack territory but went as far from the main house as he could. It wasn't until he was completely exhausted that he stopped and collapsed next to an old tall oak tree.

The shift back came slowly but sooner than he wanted. Once again in human form, he sat naked with his back against the tree. He heard his visitor before he saw her.

"Go away," he ordered and hoped she would listen.

Instead of doing as she was told, Tasha stepped into view with her hands on her hips.

"Don't you bark orders out at me! Do you know how long I have been trying to follow you?" she asked.

Adam couldn't help it. He laughed. It started with just a chuckle and grew until he had to put his hand on his stomach to calm himself down. The entire time, Tasha stood in the same pose, frustration evident on her face.

Adam waved a hand in front of his face as he gathered his senses back.

"I'm so happy you find me funny," she remarked but her lips twitched as if she was holding in her laugh.

Adam didn't want to deal with her at that moment so he turned his head and closed his eyes. "I'm not fit for company right now, Tasha. Go back to the house and I'll return shortly."

When he didn't hear any movement, he looked over. She was still there. Frustrated, he raised his voice. "I mean it! Go back to the house."

"No," she replied simply then walked forward and knelt in front of him. She lifted a hand to his face but he caught her wrist.

"I'm warning you, I do not feel like myself. Go away before I hurt you." With her so close and the feel of her delicate wrist in his grasp, he barely held onto his control. His wolf was close. It wouldn't surprise him if his eyes had started to glow.

Tasha pushed closer, brushing her knees against his. "So the big bad wolf is going to hurt the little woman?" she taunted.

Adam only grunted in response.

Tasha came even closer until she was almost straddling him. "Do your worst then."

He tried to move away, to push her away—anything—but her deliberate stare and challenge were too hard to resist. She was purposely taunting him.

"Come on. Take me if you can."

The words were barely out of her mouth when he pounced. She fell back and collided with the solid ground as his body covered hers. He slammed his mouth on hers, demanding entrance.

When she didn't open fast enough, he bit her lower lip, causing her to gasp. Adam thrust his tongue inside, dominating everything he could. The blood in his body burned and throbbed as he situated himself between her legs. His cock pressed against the zipper of her jeans as he ground himself against her, showing her that he wasn't playing games.

He ripped his mouth from hers when she pushed back against him. Adam stared down at her abused lips. Guilt flooded him immediately.

"I can't be gentle with you right now. I don't want to do it this way and hurt you."

Tasha launched herself up and attached her mouth to his neck. She sucked his skin into her mouth while running her nails down his back. He hissed and arched from the slight bite of pain.

"I don't want gentle. I want you to take me right here and now. Fuck me, Adam," she whispered in his ear.

God help him, he couldn't resist her. She had given him permission to use her. To ride her hard. And he wasn't going to pass that up.

He pushed her back down and quickly went about removing her clothes. She lifted her hips to help him pull her pants down then reached up and removed her shirt and bra as he yanked off her panties.

"You're going to have to start buying me new underwear if you keep doing that," she teased.

Adam growled and buried his face in her stomach. "Shouldn't wear any ever again." His response came out muffled.

He tried to slow himself down but he could smell the heat and juices from her sweet pussy. She was just as hot as he was. The wolf inside was almost at the surface, and the animal wanted to come out to play.

"Adam..." Tasha wriggled under him.

He pulled back and settled more firmly between her legs. Cupping her bottom, he lifted her up and brought her hot core to the tip of his hard shaft. He was going to give it to her hard but he wanted her to enjoy it also.

"Look at me," he demanded. "Watch me as I take you. As I fuck you any way I want."

Her eyes widened, her breath quickened and she nodded. His words were obviously turning her on.

Adam plunged inside with a howl, catching her scream by slamming his mouth down on hers.

Tasha's inner muscles squeezed and tried to hold him inside, causing Adam to close his eyes and wait. The peacefulness that overtook his body now that he was buried inside threatened to bring tears to his eyes.

"Adam." Tasha reached up to brush the hair of his forehead.

Adam opened his eyes and saw her smile. "It feels like home."

Tasha nodded in response to his declaration. "I feel it too."

Adam started to withdraw from her but thought better. He leaned down and kissed her with all the passion and love he felt.

Tasha opened for him immediately. When she lifted her head to deepen the kiss, he nipped her bottom lip.

"I have to move now, baby," he told her honestly.

Tasha's response was to lift her legs higher around his waist. "Then get busy."

He laughed as he pulled out and slammed back in. Her breath stuttered and he did it again. He started with long, deep strokes, trying to draw out both of their pleasures.

Anger and confusion no longer ate at him. Now it was only the need to take care of his woman.

Tasha's nails dug into his shoulders and he continued to plunge inside her, but it wasn't enough for him. He quickly left the hot haven of her body to flip her onto her stomach. She was barely in position before he grabbed her hips and thrust back inside. He rode her hard, enjoying the small sounds that were escaping her lips. When he felt her body tremble, he reached around and rubbed her clit.

"Yes," she moaned.

Adam continued to play with her until he felt his balls draw up. Knowing climax was only seconds away, he pinched her clit hard. She screamed before exploding. Adam followed her into release, his seed filling her, before they both collapsed forward.

Tasha recovered first and wiggled out from under Adam. He wrapped his arm around her as he shifted onto his side. Her sigh was enough to calm his beating heart.

"That was great," she said dreamily.

Adam laughed. "It was that, indeed."

She crawled up until she was resting her head on his chest. "Are you feeling better now?"

He couldn't resist. Adam lazily ran his hand over her bottom, delighting in the shivers he caused. "I feel great," he commented.

Tasha giggled before slapping his chest. "I meant about what happened earlier in the house."

Adam removed his hand and started to sit up. "How much did you hear?" he asked.

Tasha dropped her gaze and reached for her pants.

Adam caught her hand and pulled her into his lap. When she wouldn't look up, he gently raised her chin with his fingers.

"Tasha?"

"A lot. But your father told me the rest," she admitted.

Adam cursed and started to move her away.

"No! Adam, wait!" She wrapped her arms around his neck.

"What?" He tried to relax his body but he couldn't. He had made a fool of himself in the house. Not only that but he had probably hurt and embarrassed his father as well.

"Your father loves you. He just wanted me to make sure you were okay," she began to explain.

Adam shook his head, cutting her off. "It's not that, baby." To emphasise what he was saying, he gave her a short but sweet kiss. "I acted like a jerk."

"So...does that mean your okay with...your father?" Tasha avoided meeting his gaze as she asked.

Adam waited to answer. Was he? He knew the answer. He didn't care whom his father chose to love. A lot of weres enjoyed both male and female partners before mating. What was bothering him was that his father had hidden it from him. But Tasha deserved the truth.

"I'm okay with it. We need to talk but I just want him to be happy."

Tasha's grin brightened her face. "I'm so glad you feel that way. Everyone here is so great and...I really like Logan."

Adam nodded. "So do I."

Tasha climbed off his lap and this time he let her. "So are you ready to go back?"

As he watched her shimmer into her clothes, Adam's body wanted something completely different. "Yeah, we'd better go in before they send out a bigger search party."

Tasha hummed, smiling. "Just don't greet them the same way."

He was amused, loving the playful side she was sharing with him. "Get dressed, my little minx."

Adam held her hand the entire walk back to the house. Tasha knew he needed to talk to his dad—and after rolling around in the dirt she needed the shower—but she was looking forward to spending more time in bed with him.

She wasn't sure what was going to happen when they got back into their own territory. Here, away from everything, she could pretend Adam was hers.

They paused briefly when they came to the tree where he had shed his clothes earlier. She watched as he redressed, thinking what a shame it was to cover up all of that smooth, tanned skin. He took her hand once again and they resumed their journey back to the house.

When the house came into view, she could see her sister sitting on the back porch with Gage and Marissa. The happiness on Crystal's face was amazing and brought a smile to Tasha's face.

Adam squeezed her hand. "She's doing good."

"Yes," she agreed. "It was a good thing to bring her here. I don't know how I will ever repay you."

"Just be happy too, Tasha. That's all I want. To make you happy," he told her as he brought her hand up to her lips.

Before she could respond or even digest what he'd said, Gage stood and walked towards them. Tasha leaned up and kissed Adam's cheek. "I'll wait in your room for you."

"Thank you, Tasha." He slowly let her hand go as she walked away. When she looked back over her shoulder at him, he was still watching her with what she could almost convince herself was love.

Adam watched Tasha walk away from him, knowing she had just sealed her fate. Her coming to him and accepting him at his worst proved she had everything that was needed for not only being a mate but also a mate to an Alpha. He would do everything in his power to keep her. He would be lying if he said he wasn't already in love with her.

He waited until Gage had almost reached him before he acknowledged the other Alpha.

"You knew," he accused but without the anger he'd felt earlier.

Gage nodded and stopped in front of him. "I suspected. They still haven't *told* me, but it's not something that you miss when you are with them every day."

Adam shook his head and started towards the house. Gage easily shifted to block him. Amused, Adam lifted his eyebrow and waited.

"Before you go in there, think about what you're going to say," Gage suggested.

Adam's back stiffened automatically. He didn't take orders from anyone else. Gage must have caught his feelings because he reached out and gently laid a hand on Adam's shoulder.

"Your father is happy for the first time in months. Logan is a good man and a close friend. I just don't want to see anyone hurt." Gage looked sincere as he spoke.

"Don't worry, Gage. Now that I'm over the initial shock, I can admit that Logan is good for my father. I just want him to be happy," Adam told the other man. He couldn't seem to settle so he began to pace. "I just don't understand why he didn't tell me earlier, why he thought he had to hide it."

Gage nodded and looked back towards the house. "Well, the only way you'll get the answers is if you ask him."

Adam's gaze followed Gage's. His father and Logan had just stepped out onto the deck. His father looked uneasy. Logan's arm went immediately to his father's shoulder to show support. That simple action proved the two men had more of a bond than just sexual. Adam had known that deep down but he liked seeing that Logan would publicly comfort Christian.

"Logan won't leave your Pack," Adam whispered so only Gage's ears would pick up what he was saying.

"No, he won't. I'm sorry, Adam." After nodding, Gage turned and headed back to the house.

Christian said something to Logan then began the short walk to his son. Adam didn't meet him but waited until his father was closing in before gesturing back into the trees. Neither spoke as they drifted farther away.

When Adam felt they were far enough from the others' hearing, he turned to face Christian.

His father stopped and crossed his arms over his chest. Adam fought a smile that pulled at his lips. He'd seen that stance a thousand times as a child.

"First, I apologise for the outburst earlier. I was taken by surprise, but I didn't mean any disrespect towards you or Logan," Adam started.

Christian blinked at him and shook his head. "What?"

Adam couldn't stand still so he began to pace. Again. It seemed that since he'd moved up the ranks he was pacing more and more. He wasn't sure how to get the words he wanted to say out. After several tries, he flopped down on the grass. "I shouldn't have run off that way. I acted like a child."

His father knelt in front of him. "Yes, you did. But you're my child so that can be forgiven easily. I've wanted to tell you so many times. I didn't want you to find out like this."

"Why *didn't* you tell me? Why keep this a secret?" That was the question that kept circling in his mind.

His father sighed before answering. "You were so young when your mother died. I know you don't remember much about her."

Adam didn't understand what his mom had to do with anything. He started to ask but his father held up his hand. "Just let me get through this."

Adam nodded so he continued.

"I met Logan a couple years before your mom. We connected immediately. But when my father made a deal with the Alpha of the Pack to mate me with his daughter, I had to give him up," Christian explained.

"You were with Logan before Mom?" Adam couldn't help but interrupt.

"Yes. It was hard but I finally came out to my father. He took it much better than I could have ever hoped. When I told my father that I loved Logan, he had already made the deal. He felt bad but there was nothing he could do."

Adam opened then closed his mouth. He wanted to hear the rest.

"Things were different back then. Two male weres didn't openly date or even think about going public with a relationship with another. And I did need a wife to give the Pack pups."

"Did you see Logan when you were mated to my mom?" He had to know.

"No." Christian shook his head fiercely. "Logan left the Pack and joined this one. I told your mother the truth right after we were mated and she seemed okay with it. Even asked if I wanted to see him." Christian laughed. "Your mother was wonderful. She never made me feel bad about my feelings for Logan. After we were together for over twenty years, she went behind my back and contacted him."

Adam gasped in astonishment.

"Yes. I was quite shocked myself. She knew that I loved her, but without Logan, I was incomplete."

"What happened?" Adam's voice was just above a whisper. He had so many questions. He'd always heard how his mother always put everyone above herself. She had been one of the most unselfish and caring person anyone knew. Stories from his dad and others in the Pack were all he really had of the woman who'd given birth to him, but they had always made him feel closer to her.

"Well...Logan came to visit." Christian's eyes clouded as if he was revisiting a memory. Adam found himself scooting closer to him, wanting to share it. "At first I was so mad at her I could have strangled her. But then she calmly told both of us that we either needed to get over one another or admit our feelings out loud and in front of her." Christian met his gaze. "So we did. And do you know what your mother did?"

Adam shook his head. There was no telling.

"She kissed me."

Adam only frowned. What could he say to that? "Then?"

Christian laughed deeper than. "Then she asked Logan if he wanted to kiss me."

"He did." Adam knew somehow.

His father smiled. "He did. When we finally broke apart, we turned to your mother and her smile was as big as the state."

"She was happy about it?"

"After we kissed, she walked up just as bold as can be and kissed Logan."

Adam jolted. "What?"

"It seems after years of me talking about Logan, then getting to know him herself, she had gained feelings for him too."

It was too much. Adam jumped onto his feet and backed away. "Are you telling me that the three of you..."

His father nodded. "Until she died."

"I don't think I want to hear anymore." Adam put his hand one his stomach and turned away. It wasn't like he was new to the world of ménage. He'd even participated in a few. But they were talking about his mother here. He turned back to his dad, anger burning in his veins. "Why did you tell me this?"

"Because I wanted you to understand I am not betraying your mother. I loved her very much. And she loved both Logan and me." Christian stood and stepped closer so he could grasp Adam's shoulder. "As Alpha of the Pack, I had to hide my feelings for him. I won't hide them anymore."

Adam jerked out of his hold. "But that is exactly what you've been doing!"

"I wanted to give you time to adjust to your position. You've been worried sick about me. I have been going crazy with guilt keeping this from you."

Hysterical laughter escaped until Adam thought he'd fall over. "I thought you wanted to end your existence!"

"I'm sorry, son. I just didn't want to see disgust in your eyes when you look at me. I love you and I couldn't take that," Christian admitted emotionally. His father's eyes teared up.

Adam wiped the tears from the corners of his own eyes that the laughter had caused. "I just want you to be happy. I don't care if it's with Logan or half the men in the Pack."

His father embraced him. "Don't let Logan hear you say that."

Adam slapped his dad on the back. "You got it."

Chapter Six

True to her word, Tasha was waiting in his room when Adam went up later. He stepped inside and froze at the sight of Tasha sprawled out in his bed above the covers completely naked.

Her legs were wide open and she was playing with her sweet wet pussy.

"You might want to close the door before someone else walks by," she teased him then ran her fingers up to her clitoris and rubbed.

She moaned as he slammed the door closed. Adam fought to get his clothes off and tripped when one of his pants legs got wrapped around his ankle.

Tasha laughed and began to play with her breasts. "I'm happy to see you're in a hurry. I've been laying here forever. I had to start without you."

Now nude, Adam stood and walked to the side of the bed. "And who gave you permission to touch yourself?"

She bit her lip as she pulled on one pert nipple. "I don't believe I asked. Maybe I should be punished."

Oh, she doesn't know what she's in for now, Adam thought to himself happily. Faster than she could have stopped him, he grabbed both her wrists and slammed them above her head into the soft mattress.

He teased her lips with his. "Bad, bad girl. Now what should I do with you?"

Tasha's eyes lit with delight as he took control of her. "Whatever you want," she answered.

"Good answer, but I already was." Adam kissed one cheek then the other before moving to her forehead, eyes, and chin. She tried to stretch her body up to connect with his but he wouldn't let her.

"Kiss me," she demanded.

He tsked. "Maybe I will...later."

He flipped her onto her stomach so fast her surprised gasp was caught in her throat. He straddled her waist and held her down. "Now, let's see about this punishment."

Adam reached down and grabbed her shirt from the floor. He easily tore it in half.

"Hey! What are you doing?" she asked, trying to turn her head to see.

"You'll see," he told her as he lifted one of her wrists. She didn't struggle as he tied it to the frame of the bed. Before he tied the other wrist, he nipped the skin and felt her pulse speed up. "You like this." He chuckled.

Once her hands were secure, he rubbed his body down hers as he moved to the foot of the bed. His shirt was hanging there, so he picked it up and tore it like he had hers.

Tasha began to move under him, which turned out to help him more. He was able to tie her ankles to the bottom of the frame, using the extra material since she wasn't tall enough to reach. It left her a little wiggle room but not much.

"Now what are you going to do?" She tossed her hair to the side. "You do have a plan, don't you?"

Adam smiled as his hand came down to smack her pretty little ass.

She yelped.

"Oh yes, sweetcheeks, I have a plan. How it goes from here is determined by you." He spanked her other ass cheek.

Tasha hissed and tried to move her legs. "I was just playing about the punishment," she complained.

"I wasn't." Four more times his hand came down.

Tasha moved around but didn't tell him to stop. He straddled her upper legs and massaged her now pink bottom with his hands. "Those were for talking back to your Alpha." He pinched her skin. "These next ones are for touching yourself without permission."

Quickly his hand came down half a dozen more times. She jerked in her restraints and cried out. But Adam was a wolf shifter—he smelt her arousal.

He used two fingers to slide between her folds and spread the juices. "Oh, my naughty, naughty girl. You like that."

Tasha moaned in response as he continued to tease her.

"Now I can fuck you or..." He pressed his coated fingers against her small opening in the back.

"Oh!" She groaned loudly as he inserted just the tip of one.

"You like that?" he asked, pulling his finger out and slowly pushing it in a little deeper.

"Uh huh."

"Good." Adam withdrew again but moved up to press his erection against her. "I want to take you there. Hell, baby, I want to take you every way."

"Mmm hmm," came her muffled response.

"But I'm not going to." He moved off her and stood by the bed. "Yet."

"What?" she yelled and snapped her head around to glare at him.

Adam shrugged as he looked down at her. "I kind of like you in this position. Spread wide open for me."

She blinked several times at him, her mouth opening and closing. "Adam White, if you don't get on this bed and fuck me hard, I swear I'll... I'll hurt you," she threatened.

Adam laughed full out and started to stroke his cock. He was wound up so tight with wanting her he was already ready to explode.

"I'm not kidding," she screamed.

"Now, darling, maybe you should keep you voice down. You wouldn't want your sister to hear you and come investigate, would you?"

She growled, a low warning from the back of her throat.

"I swear when you untie me I'm going to make you pay!" She had lowered her voice but the threat was still there.

"Don't make promises you can't keep, sweetheart," he said, delighted with her. The thought of being tied down and bound for her pleasure was almost enough to have him exploding. He squeezed the base of his shaft to control his needy cock.

The look on her face was comical. Adam had no doubt she would make good on her statement but he was enjoying himself. "Now I haven't had dinner so I am just going to..."

He moved from the side of the bed, waited for her cursing to stop, then once again positioned himself between her legs. "Feast."

He bent his head and ran his tongue over her swollen sex. Tasha shuddered under him. Pushing her cheeks apart, he stabbed his tongue inside, filling his mouth with her cream.

Tasha panted and tried to push into him. His tongue lapping inside her, he used one hand to tease and pinch her clit.

She came with a low, sexy groan but he still didn't stop. Licking up her climax, he pushed two fingers deep inside her hungry pussy. The walls of her vagina gripped him and his cock jumped wanting to feel her.

Soon, he wouldn't have a choice but to come inside her or on the bed. But not yet.

He moved his tongue up and circled her puckered hole. He pushed inside, his fingers still working in and out of her pussy, getting them good and wet before he added a finger along with his tongue. He worked her back entrance open.

She shook and pleaded for him to take her. He moved his mouth and lapped around her firm, round ass checks as he used two fingers inside her anus. Oh yes, he was going to take her there.

She was so tight his fingers barely had room to move. He scissored his digits, opening her wider. Adding some spit so there wasn't any discomfort, he inserted a third finger and she wailed with need.

Not being able hold off any longer, he ripped the ties that bound her ankles from the bed. She scooted her legs up on the bed under her stomach, leaving herself open.

Adam gripped her hips and impaled her with his steel rod in one slow, long slide. Tasha screamed, convulsing around him. He had to clench his teeth as she almost pulled him over the edge. She fell face forward onto the bed.

"I'm not through with you yet," he told her, slowly pulling back. He could feel the aftershocks in her body as he moved inch by inch. He slammed back in, hard. "No one else will ever be enough for you."

Withdraw and thrust.

"Me, only me." He plunged harder and faster. "You're mine." He pounded harder. "Mine. Mine. Mine," he chanted.

"Yes! Adam, yes." She screamed as she climaxed. He didn't hold back any longer. He let himself go, each stroke more brutal than the last until he howled his own completion and emptied inside her.

* * * *

Tasha listened to the water turn off in the adjoining bathroom and sighed in pleasure. Adam had offered to carry her into the bathroom and bathe her, but she wanted to stay in bed and bask in what had just happened.

It had been the best sex of her life. She rolled onto her side where she could see the bathroom door. It had been more than sex. It had been all-consuming erotic pleasure she was sure had ruined her for all others.

But if what Adam had said during sex was true, she wouldn't have anyone else. She was his.

Her heart sped up at the thought. She closed her eyes as she thought about belonging to him. Oh, how she wished she could believe that. That he wanted to keep her. In only a few short days, she had fallen head over heels in love with him. Still, how seriously could she take seriously declarations made during sex?

"Penny for your thoughts."

Surprised, she glanced up and saw him leaning against the doorframe. She smiled and lifted the bed covers, inviting him to join her. He dropped the towel from around his waist, revealing his already hard cock. It was a beautiful sight standing tall and long from his body. She licked her lips, wanting to taste him.

He slid in next to her and wrapped his arms around her, pulling her close. "As much as I think I would enjoy what you're thinking right now by that gleam in your eye, I want you to tell me what you were thinking about so intently when I came back in the room."

She propped her chin on her hand and met his eyes. She had never been a coward and she wouldn't start now. If he didn't feel the same about her, it was better to learn that now than when they got back in the territory.

"I love you." She spoke the three most important words of her life and waited.

Adam's eyebrows lifted in surprise, but didn't say anything.

Tasha's heart fell. "Forget I said anything." She started to move away but his arms tightened around her.

"I will do no such thing." He growled. "Did you mean it?"

She glanced around the room, trying to think of a way out of what she had said.

He rolled them over until she was under him. "I asked, did you mean it?"

Knowing she had just messed everything up, she tried to blink back the tears that threatened. "I said it, didn't I?" she snapped.

Adam's mouth slammed down on hers so hard she felt his teeth cut into her lips. She opened her mouth to tell him but he didn't give her the chance. He swept his tongue inside, mating with hers.

Tasha wasn't sure what it meant but just the feel of him on top of her kissing her like the world was ending was enough to arouse her once again. She kicked at the sheets, trying to get them lowered so she could wrap herself around him.

His hands moved to help her then he was sliding inside. No foreplay or pleasantries, he just entered her body and held still.

Finally, he released her mouth to stare into her eyes. "I never believed you would fall in love with me. I thought I would have to fight to convince you."

Slowly, he withdrew before gliding back inside. "You don't know how hard it's been for me not to mate with you."

Her eyes had started to drift closed but at his declaration they popped open. "What?"

He knelt back, taking her body with him, lifting her hips as he went. This angle made every thrust inside deeper. "I love you, Tasha. I want you in my life forever."

Tears fell from her eyes, but she didn't try to wipe them away. Instead, she wrapped her arms around his shoulders and pulled herself up. Pure joy flooded her heart. He wanted her. It didn't matter anymore whether or not she was good enough for him. She wasn't going to let him go. He was just as much hers as she was his. And she would prove to him and everyone else she could take care of her mate. The man she loved.

She took over the rhythm and rode him gently. "Say it again."

He caught her chin in his fingers. "I love you."

Just those words were enough to send her over the edge. A slow, soft climax took over her body as she shuddered in his arms.

Adam gripped her hips and plunged up faster. "I love you." he said again, releasing his seed and sealing their fate.

Adam paused outside her father's door. He could hear the low hushed voices of Christian and Logan inside. They should have heard or sensed him coming but it didn't sound like they had. At least he wasn't walking in blindly this time.

He knocked softly on the door, not wanting to wake everyone else in the house. He needed to talk to his dad and it wasn't something that was going to wait.

After some rustling of clothes and who knew what else, the door opened slightly and Christian stuck his head out.

"Adam," he said surprised.

"I know it's late, but I wanted to talk to you if I could." He didn't think his father would turn him away.

Christian looked over his shoulder then back at him. "Well, Logan's here."

Adam shrugged. He'd meant what he had told his father about the two men's relationship. Now was the time to prove it. "I don't mind if he doesn't. Actually, it would be great if I could share this with him too."

Christian opened the door wider, clearly not sure but letting his son in.

Logan sat at the foot of the bed. It was obvious the two men had rushed to get dressed. Both of their clothes were very wrinkled and crooked, plus his father had buttoned his shirt wrong. Adam smiled at the other man and took a seat in the only chair in the room. "I'm sorry to disturb you so late, but I wanted to talk to you tonight. We'll be leaving in the morning."

Christian sat next to Logan and sighed deeply.

"I hope you don't feel you have to leave," Logan told him. Adam noticed as he reached out and grasped Christian's hand.

Adam shook his head before smiling widely. "It's time for me to get back to the territory and my job. Luckily, a lot of the members are vacationing, which was why I was able to leave without a lot of fuss, but I want to go home."

Both men nodded. "That's probably a good idea," his father told him.

Now was the time for the big news. Adam took a deep breath. "There's more."

Christian visibly tensed.

"I've asked Tasha to mate with me and she's accepted. We want to wait until we get back in our own territory before we go ahead. Which is the main reason we are in a hurry to return."

Christian jumped up from the bed quickly followed by Logan. "Oh, son! That is great." His father hugged him tightly.

"Congratulations!" Logan added with a slap on the back.

"Thanks. I want to give her time to plan a ceremony, but I had to tell you. Hopefully, you will come." Adam felt tears pool behind his eyes and sniffed. "Actually I would like you both to be involved."

"Both of us?" Logan asked with doubt in his voice.

Adam reached out a hand to him. When the other man accepted it, Adam gave it a good squeeze. "You've been in my life since I can remember. Now you have not only brought me my father back but have also made him the happiest I have seen him in too many years. I would be honoured if you would stand up beside me."

Logan's throat worked before tears started to fall. Christian was already wiping his own eyes and Adam couldn't hold back any longer. "I love you both. And I love Tasha and Crystal. I can't believe I am this lucky. Please say you'll be a part of my ceremony."

"Yes," his father finally answered. "Yes from both of us. We love you too."

Epilogue

The day of the ceremony, Adam was relieved his father and Logan were there to help Tasha. While the three of them were busy getting everything ready, with the help of their friends, Adam was buried deep in work.

He needed to pick a second-in-command. In the two weeks he had returned with Tasha and Crystal and moved them into his home, he'd made a lot of progress. Decision made, he was only left to announce it. He knew it would come as a shock to most of the Packs, but he felt good about it. It had been great to have a mate to talk over his choice with. Tasha had a sharp mind and understood almost too well how his mind worked.

He heard the footsteps coming down the hall before a knock came at his door.

"Enter," he grunted, knowing his time was up. He had other deals to seal today.

Christian, Logan, and Cain walked in and closed the door behind them.

"Everything's ready," his father told him.

Adam stood, smiling. "How nervous is she?"

The three laughed in unison. "Let's just say everything had better go according the plan or your mate is going to make heads roll," Logan answered.

Adam glanced at each man fondly before resting on his father. He wasn't sure if his dad realised it was the first time he'd been back into the office since before Adam had become Alpha. Maybe not, but it showed how much better Christian was doing.

"You're mate is quite the spitfire," Cain complimented.

Adam chuckled, that was saying it mildly.

Tasha had been very busy since their return. In addition to planning the mating ceremony, Tasha spent her days with Crystal helping the girl get settled, and her nights with him.

Crystal had flourished in the past weeks. She was now up to running four miles with them and had even started talking to other non-shifters over the Internet, setting up a support group. He couldn't be more proud of his two ladies.

"How's the search for your top Enforcer?" Cain asked, walking to the bar on the side of the room. He poured four drinks before passing them out.

As second-in-command and top Enforcer of his Pack, Cain knew how hard a position it could be to fill.

"Actually, I was just thinking about that. I made my decision," he told them. "I am just waiting to see if he will accept."

When he didn't elaborate, the other men laughed.

"Well, with two Alphas and two seconds in the room, I guess that's about the best we are going to get," Logan joked.

Adam swirled the brown liquid in his glass and took a drink. "It will work out, but first, I have a woman to make mine."

"She's already yours," his father told him, walking up and throwing his arm around him.

"Yes, she is. But I want to announce it to the world," Adam said before draining his drink.

"I told you, man. There's nothing like having a mate," Cain said smugly.

"Yeah, yeah, yeah." Adam rolled his eyes. "Then let's get this show on the road."

He left the office and made his way to the backyard. He smiled at the transformation the area had undergone. Tasha had worked hard and it had paid off.

His father and Logan walked ahead of him, leaving him to stand on the back porch with Cain.

"Was Tony able to get away from the city?" he asked his friend.

Cain shook his head. "No. I'm not sure what is going on with him, but he sounded strange last night when we spoke."

Adam lifted a brow in question.

"He wouldn't tell me what was going on. Said he had something to look into then he'd call." Cain's face tightened as he spoke.

"I'm sure he'll be okay," Adam said in support.

Cain released a breath before nodding. "I understand the importance of coming out of hiding. Sometimes, though," he sighed, "I think it will do more harm than good."

Adam agreed. It was one reason he felt so strongly about bringing his second in. He looked over the crowd and his gaze settled on the man in question.

Adam nodded and the other man started walking to them.

Cain must have seen him at the same time because he growled. "What the hell is he doing here?"

Adam knew it was time to come clean. "I invited him."

Cain turned towards him. "Why?"

Adam met his friend's eyes. "You're not the only one who is worried about what our coming out will mean. I want to be able to protect my Pack."

Understanding dawned on Cain's face. "I see."

Larry reached them and held a hand out, first to Adam then Cain. Cain was clearly reluctant to take it, but he did.

"I'm glad you could make it," Adam told him honestly.

"I would like to speak with you more about your offer. If I decide to accept, it will be important to get to know the Pack," Larry stated.

Cain cleared his throat. "I'd better go find Emily."

Adam watched his best friend walk away before he turned back to the man he hoped would become family. "Sorry about that."

Larry shrugged off his apology. "I understand. Cain went through a lot with his mate."

"Still, if you take the job you may get a lot of flak," Adam warned. He wanted the man to accept with his eyes open.

Larry laughed, surprising him. "I left my old Pack because I didn't like the way it was run. I don't think I'll have that problem here."

Adam was relieved. The pieces were falling into place.

"I should have told everyone who I suspected was responsible for the attacks. I was just so used to not having any back-up," Larry continued. "I've never had anyone I could trust."

Adam understood what Larry was talking about. From what he knew of Larry's old Alpha, the man ran his Pack like a military unit instead of a family. It was because of Larry that they had been able to capture the attacker from months earlier without Cain's mate Emily becoming his next victim.

Larry had followed the man he suspected back to Emily. He had reached them before the man could harm her. Before Cain could get to her.

While it was a blessing Larry had been suspicious and followed the man, saving Emily in the process, it was still a sore spot for Cain.

Emily was his mate and he should have been able to protect her. Adam knew it was more of his pride being stung than anything else. Cain was known as the best and most efficient Enforcer from any Pack.

But Adam knew his friend. Cain would come around. Everyone would. Adam felt that Larry would be the perfect addition to his Pack. He'd shown he was loyal and had a sense of rightness that Adam wanted.

Larry had indeed proved himself.

Soon after Larry had saved Emily, he'd gone Rogue. That didn't bother Adam. Larry was just looking for a place to fit in. Adam was hopefully offering him that.

"I hope you come to trust me," Adam told him and held out his hand. Larry accepted it.

"I believe I can."

The music started in the background and Adam grinned. "Now I have a woman to claim."

His new friend smiled and slapped him on the back. "Better hurry. I'm told women don't like to wait."

Adam was still chuckling as he made his way to the altar to take his place. Yes, all the pieces were indeed coming together. His Pack Territory would be just fine

.

About the Author

Crissy Smith lives in Texas with her husband, daughter, and three Labrador retrievers. The three dogs love to curl up under her computer desk and nap while she writes. It doesn't leave a lot of room for her but what's a woman to do?

When not writing or reading, she enjoys hunting, camping and shooting. But she has a girly side too and is addicted to pedicures and coffee.

She has been writing since she was a teenager and still loves everything to do with the paranormal. Her stories and characters all have a place in her heart. She loves the alpha male, the dominant werewolf, or the Master vampire which find their way in most of her books.

Learn more about the characters she has created at her website where they have their very own page. It will be updated from time to time to let you know what's going on with them. Also you can find out who will be in the next book.

Crissy Smith loves to hear from readers. You can find her contact information, website details and author profile page at http://www.total-e-bound.com.

Total-E-Bound Publishing

www.total-e-bound.com

Take a look at our exciting range of literagasmic™
erotic romance titles and discover pure quality
at Total-E-Bound.

www.ingramcontent.com/pod-product-compliance
Lightning Source LLC
Chambersburg PA
CBHW032025240626
47154CB00003B/785